VOODOO LUCY SERIES
BOOK FIVE
NIGHT TERRORS

VOODOO LUCY SERIES
BOOK FIVE
NIGHT TERRORS

VITO ZUPPARDO

Copyright © 2022 Vito Zuppardo

All rights reserved.

Publisher's Note: This book is a work of fiction. Names, characters, businesses, organizations, places, events, and incidents are the product of the author's imagination or are used in a fictional manner.

No part of the book may be reproduced, scanned, or distributed in any printed or electronic format without permission.

A special thanks to my wife Diane, for the inspiration of her original art for the cover of this book. I will always feel your presents as if you never left my side.

WHAT READERS ARE SAYING

VOODOO LUCY SERIES

Reviewed in the United States on December 18, 2021
Verified Purchase

Wow, but this book I started this morning and Vito I can tell you I could not put it down. I read fast but this story got better the more I read and I just was so unhappy when I saw those two words "the end". I have loved the Lucy series and I really liked Darby right off. She was. a great one to add because she did make the story. I would highly recommend this entire series if any of you who not read any. You are missing a treat. Lucy makes you want to be like her and help others who are unfortunately in a bad spot. So buy the series and enjoy your weekend.

Fantastic book…
Reviewed in the United States on December 16, 2021
Verified Purchase

If you have read any of the books, Vito has written, you were blessed. This book, was very enjoyable .. we love Voodoo Lucy, and always waiting until the next book in the series comes out. True Blue Detective Series also is fantastic. I highly recommend you get to know Ms. Lucy …

Well written with believable characters
Reviewed in the United States on January 8, 2022
Verified Purchase
As a native Louisianian, I can truly appreciate the accuracy of the details about New Orleans and the rest of our fair state as well as the people in it. The good, the bad and the corrupt.

This a Must read
Reviewed in the United States on December 30, 2021
Verified Purchase
I have read all of the Voo-Doo lucy series-Mirror of Lies is the Best one yet- If you have not read this series-you are missing out on a great series. I am glad I read these books in order-that way I can keep up with the characters.

Get Vito Zuppardo's Starter Library FREE
Sign up for the no-spam newsletter and get FREE bonus books.
www.vitozuppardobooks.com/newsletter

ALSO BY VITO ZUPPARDO

True Blue Detective series
True Blue Detective
Crescent City Detective
Vieux Carré Detective
Street Justice
Escape To New Orleans
Two Kinds of Justice
Irish Bayou
The Auction House

Voodoo Lucy series
Tupelo Gypsy
Revenge
Club Twilight
Mirror of Lies
Night Terrors

Lady Luck series
Alluring Lady Luck
Tales of Lady Luck

<u>WANT MORE?</u>

START THE VOODOO LUCY

and

TRUE BLUE DETECTIVE SERIES

AT THE END OF THIS BOOK.

CHAPTER 1

Lucy Jones had finally moved out of her French Quarter apartment over the beauty salon on Royal Street. The only things left in the apartment were an old bed and mattress. Her intentions were to turn the room into a revenue producer by flipping it to inventory for Club Twilight, Lucy's after-hours business—entertainment for the rich, political powers of the city and the outright sexually deprived men and women in her black book.

It was time to move on to the prestigious Lakefront community of New Orleans. It was a purchase she made a month ago and had a hard time coming to terms with, being an impulse decision. It wasn't about the money. She had legit money banked to pay cash, but guilt followed Lucy. No one in her family had ever owned a house—much less one this size. Her father's words were embedded in her mind. *You were born into a poor family and will die poor like the rest of us.* Edgar, her father, reminded Lucy and her mother they were poor white trash. He had drilled into them the idea not to expect anything more out of life.

The Lakefront mansion was a residential area where "new" money lived. They weren't the "old" money people who lived in Antebellum mansions in the Garden District. Those people never worked a day in their life and got their wealth the old-fashioned way—by inheritance.

Lucy's trusted bodyguard, Darby, now a live-in companion, dropped the last box in the bedroom closet. Darby turned into a godsend, doing everything for Lucy. She was her personal driver, the voice of reasoning, bodyguard, and sometimes would make a questionable attempt at cooking. The saying applied *don't quit your day job*. Cooking dinner wasn't Darby's forte.

In earlier days, a move was easy. The clothes on Lucy's back and a small handbag carried her possessions.

Running cons in Tupelo with her father was not the life she wanted, but it was the life she was forced to live. A break came when Edgar sent Lucy and Wanda to New Orleans. They jumped at the chance to leave Tupelo and never questioned how he knew Vivien and arranged for them to work in the salon. They went, expecting him to follow a week later.

Edgar was the king of cons, and the last one he pulled was on Lucy and Wanda. He got them out of his life and never met them in New Orleans.

Taking over Vivien Bluff's business was natural for Lucy. She worked her way from running glasses of champagne to the rich in the salon to managing where the real money was made. Two tiny apartments above the salon made more money in one night than the salon made all week. Vivien, called the "French Quarter Madam" by her clients, kept their names in her black book safely at Club Twilight, her after-hours business. The ladies of Club

Twilight were the moneymakers who paid the bills and did not have Vivien want for anything.

Now, things were different. Lucy was known as a businesswoman on the board of the French Quarter Merchant Association and was recently elected to the New Orleans City Council. She was well-liked by most—especially the people in her black book.

It wasn't until Lucy took control of Club Twilight and the black book and studied the names that to her surprise, she saw her father Edgar's name. Not only was he a customer of Vivien's after-hour business, but he was also a pimp earning a commission. Edgar had spent a lot of time in New Orleans, coming home later to brag about the cons he ran in the French Quarter.

The book showed Edgar was paid a fee to bring men and occasionally women to Vivien. He often talked about the con he ran on men dressed in suits--watching for name tags from a convention or checking coats for logo pins on the collar. These easy signs they were conventioneers and wanted to party.

Vivien never mentioned Edgar being a customer and a pimp. Like Lucy, Vivien had a lot of secrets, and she knew how to keep them to herself.

CHAPTER 2

An unmarked van backed into the garage, and the overhead doors were closed. It was not ideal for getting Vivian's heavy old safe to the bedroom closet. The best way was the front entrance on a hand truck and a lot of muscle pulling and pushing up the stairway. Lucy wanted to hide the van and crew from curious neighbors, so the garage, which led into the house with many turns through rooms and the back stairs, was the best way—but not the easiest.

She called the content of cash, jewelry, and diamonds her emergency fund, and it was twice what most made in a year. Another vehicle arrived and parked in the spacious garage. It carried racks of clothes, including some with store tags, showing they had never been worn. The mission was accomplished, and soon all evidence of anything moving in and out of the garage was gone. They left Lucy to arrange her personal items.

It was a little after eleven that night when Darby stopped talking Lucy's arm off—and headed downstairs to her new pool house residence.

Giving off a broad smile, Darby's eyes sparkled. "We're

like sisters of a secret society." She flipped the light switch off. "Good night."

The hall light reflected Darby standing in the doorway. "Does that mean I can take you off the payroll? Since we're like sisters?"

"Let's not get crazy." Darby's voice echoed from down the hall.

It was an exhausting day, and Lucy finally crawled into bed. She plopped her head down on a soft pillow that gave off that fresh linen smell. It only took a few turns to get comfortable, and she drifted off to sleep.

A glowing streetlight peeked through a crack in the drape. Lucy wasn't sure of the time, but it must have been the middle of the night. She buried herself in the pillows and tried to shut her mind off from all the things she needed to do the next day. It worked until she was frightened by the weight of a man on top of her. He had one hand over her mouth and the other around her throat.

He whispered, "My orders are to kill you if demands are not met."

Rapidly her mind wondered how this person entered the house without tripping the alarm. If she screamed, could Darby get to the bedroom before she took her last gasp? She flipped around the bed, barely audible.

"I can't breathe."

She felt the pressure come off her throat.

"If you scream. It will be the last thing you ever hear."

She was sure it was a man's voice.

Lucy was a professional on how to observe. Her father preached the gospel of discernment ever since he took her on the road for their first father and daughter scam. The first thing was to observe the surroundings, look at the mark for tattoos or scars, and pay attention to their voice. It was something she thought she'd never need to know.

This was an attack, and the surroundings were her own house. It was a bold move for anyone to make. Lucy applied the same principles. Do you know the person? Most of all, keep them talking. All she had to go on was a whisper in the dark. Not recognizing the voice, she knew waiting for the perfect opportunity was the best move. Pelting him with questions—doing anything to stall for time. There was no reply.

The entire time he was on top, she wiggled to the edge of the mattress. "What do you want? Money, sex, what?"

Lucy had kept a knife tucked between the mattress and box spring as a teenager. She never had to use it but slept better knowing it was available. Moving to New Orleans and teaming up with Vivien allowed her to save money. To protect herself and the working girls of Club Twilight, she afforded a specially made mattress.

A seamstress who made many of Lucy's clothes cut pockets into both sides of the mattress. It was the perfect place for the women of the night to hide a weapon of choice: easy access with a wide pocket and no possibility of a struggle when pulling it out. A woman Lucy trusted came up with the design. A hardwood box fit inside the pocket allowing access to the weapon even if someone rolled over the top of the mattress.

Her fingers crawled the sheets to the edge of the

mattress the entire time, whispering to her attacker. "Come on, talk to me? If not sex or money, what do you want?"

Lucy got him to relax and promised she would not scream. The pressure let off her body. Her fingers felt the pocket at the side of the mattress. If she pulled the 38-snub nose revolver, she had to be ready to put three rounds squarely into the man's chest.

A few moments later, her hand was on the gun.

"Where do you think you're going?" He pulled her by the waist to the center of the bed. The gun clutched in her hand and slipped out of the pocket just as it was designed.

It startled Lucy even more than when she first discovered him in her bed. It was the first time he spoke, and he knew her name.

So—this is not a random break-in of a mansion on the lake with the fancy cars out front, she thought. *This asshole knows me.*

A message from Juan Vargas. Felipe is dead." Lucy was sure she could not place the voice.

She wiggled the best she could, but his size overpowered her. "Who are you?"

"You don't get to ask questions." He paused. "Juan Vargas is taking over the drug business in New Orleans. We expect you to help with the police and your political connections."

Lucy squeezed the butt of the gun and tightened her finger on the trigger. "I'm not washing Vargas's money."

"We're not asking. You're out the drug business and money laundering."

He was on his knees with his body across Lucy's feet.

NIGHT TERRORS

She arched upward, giving her a little breathing room. "What are you willing to pay me for my connections?"

"What we're paying?" He laughed. "You do what we say, and you get to live. One step out of line, and you'll get two to the head."

"Those are Juan Vargas's orders?" Lucy had to keep him talking and learn much before she blew his guts out. Her former girlfriend, Stella, told her about crime scenes. Blood will shower as much as ten feet. She quickly pictured blood and body matter sprayed, covering her beautiful bed, custom sheets, and probably the walls too.

"That's not Vargas's orders. It came from Tony Bozzano."

"Bozzano is partnering up with a Colombian Drug Lord?" Lucy got most the information needed.

"It was Bozzano's idea. He wanted Felipe out, and you? He'll allow you to keep living—until he has no more use for you," the man said, leaning back chuckling. "Didn't see that one coming—huh, Lucy?"

"Why not address this at my office?" Lucy's eyes shifted, and she did her best to adjust to the dark room, making sure he was directly in front of her. "Instead, you break into my house in the middle of the night. Why?"

"Bozzano wants you to know he means business," the thug said, giving Lucy a little more freedom of her legs. "Me sitting in your bed proves he can take you out at any time." He let off another irritating laugh. "Now there is no confusion. Take the demand seriously, or you're dead."

Lucy lifted the gun and pumped three into the man's chest. The impact flipped him off the bed.

"Didn't see that coming—huh?" Lucy sat up as tears ran down her face. "Darby!" She screamed.

It didn't take long for Darby to come running upstairs, "Lucy!" she screamed from the landing. Then she went silent and tiptoed through the exercise room into the bathroom. With a Glock pointed in line with her body for a perfect shot in the dark, she scanned the bedroom from the doorway. The image of Lucy came through clearly in her night goggles—Lucy sitting up in the bed, her gun pointed, in the darkness.

"Lucy, are you okay?" Darby flipped the light on.

"Is he dead?" Lucy asked.

CHAPTER 3

THE FOLLOWING MORNING LUCY woke up to a coffee aroma coming from the kitchen. Adjusting her silky gown, she slipped on a matching robe and fastened the satin tie tightly around her waist. The back stairway led directly to the kitchen, where she found Darby pouring two cups of coffee.

"Good morning, Princess," Darby said, standing in her traditional nightclothes: gym shorts and a faded Jazz Fest T-shirt. Darby never claimed to be a girly girl. Most of the time, she shopped in the men's department. Button-down shirts, tight jeans, and combat boots were her style.

"Good morning," Lucy said, working up a smile.

Darby placed two cups of coffee on the round glass table overlooking the pool, and they sat.

She gave a peripheral glance Lucy's way. "Well, how was your first night in the big house?"

"It was good. It seems like a quiet neighborhood. What? Why are you staring at me?"

Darby was slow to respond. "Do you want to talk about the elephant in the room?"

"What elephant?"

"For starters, the three bullet holes in your bedroom wall." Darby did her best to control her voice from being demanding. If not, it could quickly turn into a shouting match that she'd lose.

"And what are you doing with night goggles?"

"You expect me to jump out of bed in the dark? Run around the house and turn on the lights so I can find my target?" Darby took a deep breath. "I protect you—that's what I do. Don't ask about goggles, the guns, or anything else I use to protect you."

"How secure is this house?"

"Don't do that," Darby pounded the table, causing coffee to spill on the glass.

Lucy gave off her usual innocent look when she didn't want to talk about something. Then shot back. "What?"

"There are three .38 slugs in your wall. How do you explain that?"

"I don't intend to explain. I had a dream, that's all."

"When you shoot a gun off in the bedroom at nothing, it's not a dream. That's your night terrors, and you need to get help."

"Darby, it was real. I didn't know I shot the gun until you busted in the room. Bozzano threatened me."

"You need to see your doctor." Darby cleaned the coffee off the table and freshened up their cups. "Are you taking your meds?" There was no reply. "I'll take that as a no."

Lucy pulled Darby by the shirt when she passed. "Again, I am asking. How secure is this house?"

"This place is protected like a palace. You better come

NIGHT TERRORS

with an army of men, or you're not getting any further than the front gates. Why do you ask?"

Giving her a side glance. "Check into a private patrol," Lucy said. "Someone to sit in the driveway dusk to dawn."

"Lucy! You have cameras facing the front and back at every angle. As well as motion detection. As it is, I caught the motion detector twice last night before the thirty-second delay triggered. Probably a cat from the neighbor's yard."

"Don't assume—let the alarm go off." Lucy pushed the issue forward.

"You had night terrors, again." Darby did her best to defuse any fear Lucy might have. "Just a dream."

"It is a big deal when I have a crazy nightmare," Lucy sipped her coffee, looking over the cup at Darby. "I learned a long time ago to pay attention to my dreams. Things may not happen as I pictured, but in the end, someone will die."

Lucy stepped back into the kitchen and returned with her purse to break the tension. She dug out her cellphone, then the calendar. That was Lucy. She would stop an argument just by focusing on something else, which meant she didn't want to talk about the issue.

Lucy rattled off her appointments for the day while Darby took notes.

"Is that the order of your meetings?" Darby questioned. "That will make two trips across town in heavy traffic."

Darby recognized Lucy's glare. The type where her eyes and mind drifted as she spoke. "We're going to make a surprise visit on Mr. Bozzano and Rosa Cruz."

"Is that wise to visit Rosa?" Darby shot her a look. "Should I call ahead?"

"Then it wouldn't be a surprise, would it?"

It was a tone you didn't want to question, and Darby did not. "Surprise visit, it is."

Darby sat in the SUV an hour later, waiting for Lucy in the circle drive. She stepped from the front entrance in tight black leather pants, a white silk blouse, and a black waistline jacket that fit perfectly, showing her figure.

Holding the car door, Darby gave a smile. "No dress and matching umbrella, today?"

"Not today. I'm going for the comfortable image."

Darby's grin grew wide. "Black leather pants with a matching vest and a white silk blouse. You look like Cat Woman. You're going for a 'kick ass' day."

"You watch too many superhero movies," Lucy said, sliding into the back seat.

Darby glanced at her in the rearview mirror. "Say what you want. With that outfit, they will be eating out of your hand—man or woman. You're sexy."

"Don't make a big deal out of it, Darby. I'm just going comfortable." She sighed in irritation. "First stop—City Hall for a quick meeting."

"Yeah, that's what you always say." Darby pulled from the driveway. "It's never quick."

CHAPTER 4

Darby dropped Lucy curbside and she took the thirty-two steps leading to the front entrance of City Hall. With a quick smile to the security guard, he waved Lucy through screening. She reached for the door handle of the old, faded steel door and opted to take the stairs to her office that morning. It was the only exercise Lucy got when wearing the right shoes. Walking to restaurants and shopping in the French Quarter was considered exercise, but it wasn't like climbing stairs. Lucy made it to the third floor. Heavy breathing indicated she had to do it more often.

Early mornings at City Hall were busy, and the hallways were flocked as people rushed to work, and others waited for the permit office to open. It was the worst floor on which to have the City Council's offices. Lucy weaved among people coming towards her in the narrow hallway. With their faces buried in their cell phones, she had to watch the oncoming walkers or risk a collision.

A voice came from behind. "Good morning, Lucy."

She recognized the soft-spoken woman as she reached her office door. The first thought that ran through her mind was, *damn, I was so close. Two seconds quicker, I would have been inside with the door closed behind me.* But she didn't.

Lucy gave a slight head turn. "Good morning, Stella."

"Lucy," Stella said, offering a smile and went in for an unwelcomed kiss. Stella caught her on the cheek. "It's been how long?"

"It is really nice seeing you, Stella, but I am late."

"I never expected this from you, Lucy."

"What?"

"Remember I helped you get elected, held your hand when you shook down to your toes before making the acceptance speech."

"Yeah, Stella, I owe it all to you." She turned the handle and opened the office door. "Nice seeing you." The door closed before Stella could say another word.

She walked directly to her private office, bypassing the secretary, and closed the door. Taking a deep breath, she flipped her purse on the chair. *What a way to start the morning, and to top it off, I run into Stella?* She beat herself up for not being more pleasant to her longtime friend. They were lovers who broke up, and there was no need to be rude. Plus, a cop with many connections was someone good to have in your back pocket.

A slight knock at the door then it opened. "That man in the waiting area is for you," the secretary said. She worked for the three council members who utilized the secretary since they were not there every day.

"I don't have any appointments this morning," Lucy

said, sitting behind her desk. "Are you sure he wants to see me?"

"He said it's important and had to see you but wouldn't explain."

Lucy's shook her head, "Don't they all say that?"

"What do I tell him?"

"You tell him I'm late for a council meeting."

"And?"

"Come get him in three minutes."

The secretary returned with the man quickly. Lucy gestured for him to sit, and he introduced himself as John Davis, a member of the Merchant Association.

He was quickly cut off. "I don't discuss French Quarter business in this office." Lucy preferred to keep conversations to City Hall business. It was an old building, and there were too many listening ears in the halls.

Lucy never could determine nationalities and was sure his real name was not John Davis. There were white people and black people in her book in the south, where she grew up. This tan- skinned man had opened a business in the French Quarter, and he could have been from any part of South America. She let his American name slide, brushing it off. Anyone investing money and time in a French Quarter business was a good merchant to her.

"What can I do for you?"

The man's eyes watered. "I can't bring this up in a merchant meeting."

Lucy walked the office in frustration. The man looked desperate, and his hand shook even though he held onto his knee to control the movement. His feeling was apparent, and it hit home with Lucy. She'd been in that position, feeling hopeless as if the weight of the world were on her shoulders. They sat next to each other, and Lucy gave her undivided attention. He had just told her about his daughter befriending a girl at school when the door opened.

"I'm sorry, Madam Councilwoman. You're late for your meeting."

"Tell them to start without me."

The woman stood confused, and her eyes shifted from Lucy to John.

"It's complicated. I'll call you when Mr. Davis is ready to leave."

With a roll of her eyes, the woman closed the door behind her.

Lucy encouraged John to continue and patted his hand.

He explained his daughter recently came to live with him but offered no details and didn't speak of a wife. Lucy picked up on it, and her con artist radar taught her to attend to the little details he didn't reveal.

Lucy was skeptical of most people when first meeting them, but John Davis jumped off the proverbial page at her. Then he added that the daughter's name was Jane.

Beth Wiggins gravitated towards Jane at school ever since the first day. Beth's father picked them up one rainy day from school.

Lucy, always short on patience, told him to get to the point.

One day after school, Beth showed Jane a room she stumbled across in the garage. A storage locker. Once inside, another door opened six steps down to a mud floor.

John held Lucy's hand tighter. "My daughter said the mud floor room was stacked with wooden boxes, and some lids were open, exposing rifles. She couldn't identify the weapons but combed through the internet and matched them to rocket launchers and fully automatic weapons. That and an uncountable number of boxes of explosives."

Lucy pulled away from his hand. "Why did you come to me?"

"I heard you can fix things," he replied.

"This is none of your business, and I have no intentions to get involved," she took a deep breath. "Go to the police."

"Ms. Lucy, I'm not the type of person that can go to the police. They will think I was involved in some way, and I'd be profiled as an arms dealer."

"Just explain. Like you told me."

"It doesn't work that way. Where I come from, I would be a suspect, and the police would think it's some arms deal gone bad."

That was the opportunity Lucy was waiting for. "Just where are you from?"

There was a long pause. "Cali."

A cocked head-side look showed her confusion.

"It's in Colombia," he said. "Cali, Valle del Cauca, Columbia."

Lucy bit on her lip. Her mind ran rapidly, wondering why a man from Colombia, the drug central of the world, would show up at her door.

"I know some police, if that would help."

"No!" He stood. "Sorry to bother you."

Before Lucy could say another word, John was at the

door. He turned the doorknob. "I hope I can trust you not to repeat any of this information." Then the door shut behind him.

Not able to accomplish what she scheduled that morning, a frustrated Lucy left by way of the stairs back down.

Darby was alerted Lucy's exit was at the side stairs. She stood eyeballing everyone that came close to Lucy when she passed through a crowd of smokers at the exit. Her attention focused on Lucy as if she were someone of importance that needed protection.

Making her way, Lucy's fanned her face for fresh air cutting through the smoke. "Does everyone smoke? When do they work?" Lucy said to Darby as she held the back door open to the SUV.

"How did it go?"

"I got ambushed by some merchant who thinks there is an arms dealer in the French Quarter." She made a face and slipped into the back seat.

"Where to?" Darby asked, pressing the ignition button.

"While I am pissed off, let's go pop in on Rosa Cruz."

"I still don't think that is a good idea."

"Just drive."

Darby peeked in the rearview mirror to Lucy's solemn cold stone face. Lucy peered out the tinted windows with barely a blink. Darby drove, keeping her eyes focused on the road. She learned early on never to speak out a second time after being shot down by her boss.

CHAPTER 5

In New Orleans, there is a mixed bag of homes in neighborhoods. One minute you could pass rows of million-dollar Antebellum homes, then turn the corner and go one block down to rows of shotgun houses.

The Ninth Ward was well-kept. It was miles away from the million-dollar homes on the boulevard, but people were proud to call it home. Like most communities over the years, people sometimes failed to keep up their property whether because of money, age, or death. That's when Felipe bought up the neighborhood. Over time he purchased most of the property, labeling it his Shanty Town fortress.

Felipe lived on the block. His family and crew occupied many homes on the street. The one on the corners and two on the block were for his bodyguards. No one would make a surprise visit on Felipe's home turf.

Darby pulled the black SUV to the curb in front of Felipe's house and met three men with hands on the guns stuck behind their oversized belt buckles. Darby didn't come unprepared. Her Glock was out of the holster on her lap and her finger was on the trigger. She sized the men, height, and weight. Sure, the bullets in the chamber would penetrate the SUV door and kill the one closest. The second and third person could be a challenge.

The rear tinted window came down halfway. Lucy reached out with her hand. "Slow down, cowboy. The last thing I want to do is tell Felipe I had to kill a few of his boys."

Their hands tightened around the holstered guns.

"I come in peace—I am Lucy Jones."

"I know who you are, Ms. Lucy," one man said, easing his hand off the gun.

The window went down all the way. A gun pointed caught him off guard. "You see, while your gun is tucked behind that five-dollar Tijuana belt buckle, we already have the jump on you. I can take one of you out. Darby may or may not kill the other two, but for sure, one of you." She motioned with her head for Darby to step out.

The driver's door opened slowly. "I'm coming out," Darby said. Then her gun whipped out from behind the door.

"See, we can take two of the three of you down. Who feels lucky that you will be the one standing after we start blasting?"

Lucy motioned for Darby to point her gun down. Reluctantly, she did.

"I didn't come to start a war. Just to talk to Rosa."

What appeared to be the lead man stepped forward and then motioned for the others to stay. He returned from the house, and made a hand motioned to Lucy to follow him.

Her purse and gun were taken and felt around the waist. She's clean," one thug said.

"Darby, stay put."

"Lucy! That's not a good idea."

"So you have said." Lucy gave an over-the-shoulder look. "I am fine. Should I not come out, don't stop firing until they are all dead."

She disappeared from the view of Darby in front of three men and walked into the house.

Rosa sat in the courtyard around a fire pit primarily for a show—it was far too warm for heat. The area was draped with flowers overflowing from large clay pots. With the vivid colors of reds, yellows, and purple, the rear looked far better than the front of the house.

Lucy tried to break the ice. "Who's got the green thumb?"

"My gardener," Rosa shot back. "What brings you here uninvited?"

Lucy studied Rosa's eyes. She was peering at something behind her.

After a deep breath, Lucy gave her a smile. Then took a seat across from the pit, looking directly at Rosa. "I would think twice before your partner in crime tries to take me out."

"Why!" Rosa stood. "You going to pull some of that Voodoo shit on us?" Pulling a blanket, she exposed an Uzi. "I'll shred you and your Voodoo curse."

Lucy, shaking inward, tried not to show her anxiety. She did what she did best and smiled. "Somehow, I think your husband will have your head if something happens to me. Remember, Felipe ordered my protection, and if not, he has to find someone to wash a million dollars a month of his drug money."

Rose flopped down on the chair, the Uzi across her lap. "What do you want, Voodoo Lady?"

"I have night terrors."

"Please! You come crying to me because you had a nightmare?"

Lucy gave a bone-chilling stare. In her world, her dreams were the reality of the coming times. It might not be today, but it could be tomorrow.

Rosa's eyes showed interest. "So, what was your nightmare?"

"Someone is going to kill Felipe."

"No way. He's better protected in jail than on the outside."

They talked for a while, and Lucy gave her as much information as possible. The last thing she wanted to discuss was that in her nightmare Tony Bozzano planned the hit.

Lucy asked for her name to be added to the prison's visitor list. But, before she could finish, Rosa hit her with the unexpected.

"No need to go see Felipe."

"Rosa, I need to talk to him, and he has to know my dreams are real."

"You don't understand. Felipe will be home in two days."

Lucy's eyes blinked rapidly, much like she did when hit with a surprise. "What?"

"His attorney found information, and the judge will consider his release tomorrow. That million dollars for you to wash next month—might be short. Get my drift? It takes a lot of cash to walk away from the sentence he had."

Lucy shook her head. "No judge will risk that."

Rosa gave a smirk. It was one Lucy had grown to hate in the few meetings with the Kingpin's sister. "When it comes to money, Lucy…" She paused. "People will do almost anything. Let me re-phrase that. When it comes to money, people *will* do anything." She laughed at Lucy as she walked out of the courtyard. "Stop in anytime. Keep me updated on your night terrors."

Bewildered and walking much like a zombie, Lucy nodded to Darby when she reached the porch. With Darby holding the door open, Lucy slipped into the back seat.

"You okay, boss? You're looking a little—"

"Just drive, Darby." Lucy's insides shook. Her hands held tightly to her legs to keep them steady.

Darby sneaked a look in the rearview mirror, then built the courage to ask. "Where to?"

"Bozzano's," Lucy said through her teeth, hardly opening her mouth.

A grin came across Darby's face. *Another surprise visit?* It ran through her mind, but she kept it to herself.

CHAPTER 6

Darby drove the SUV in the usual heavy traffic of cars, tour buses, and eighteen-wheelers loaded down with vegetables heading to the French Market. She recognized Lucy's deep funk that came because of a meeting that apparently didn't go well with Rosa. She had seen Lucy's process to shake her mood—eyes twitching, a deep stare out the window at virtually nothing in the sky. It was Lucy who would have to break the silence first, and she did.

"Hold off on Bozzano," Lucy said, her voice loud at the direction of the front seat. "Head to Royal Street."

Darby didn't question the change and made the first U-turn possible. Then turned onto Royal Street. She drove slowly, waiting for further direction, and it came.

"John Davis Fabrics on Royal and Saint Philip."

Again without questioning, Darby headed the SUV in that direction. Coming in the back way of the French Quarter, they were only a few blocks away. Stopping at the corner she pulled to the curb in an area labeled Truck Zone.

"Want me to come in?"

Lucy didn't answer, then opened the car door, and got out.

Inside she spotted John's wife from a merchants' meeting, and Lucy acknowledged her with a nod as she rearranged colorful bolts of vivid fabric stacked on tables.

"Can I help you, Ms. Lucy?" She asked.

"Here to talk with, John," she replied and bypassed her, seeing an office to the rear of the store. She knocked but didn't wait for approval to go in and opened the door.

"What's the address?"

John turned from his desk chair. "What address?"

"Do I have to spell it out for you?" Lucy shot him a look. "Your problem with your daughter's school friend?"

"I don't want to be involved," John said, getting up and closing the door.

"You come to me with a problem to fix. But you don't want to be involved?" Lucy stepped forward, and John's chair on casters backed him against a file cabinet. "It doesn't work that way."

Lucy's anxiety quickly shot upward, still not over her last meeting that had met resistance.

"I want names, addresses, and pictures of the weapons." It was a demanding tone uncommon for Lucy.

A shaky voice replied he didn't think he could get that information.

Lucy stuck her foot on the leather seat of the chair between John's legs. "Then don't ever come to me to fix something. Ever!" Lucy stormed out of the office, slamming the door and turning heads as she paraded through the store and out the front door.

"Let's go see Bozzano," she said, getting in the car's back seat.

Without a word, Darby drove a few blocks to Chartres Street and parked in front of the French Market fruit stand—a facade for the Bozzano enterprise.

Lucy knew the routine. She picked up some fruit and looked into the camera attached to a rusted hanging light fixture that had more than served its time. Shortly later, Salvador "Big Sally" Ricci, Mr. Bozzano's longtime bodyguard, came through a door disguised by a painted mural wall. He and Lucy became friends over the years, but they both knew they were using each other for information. She sweet-talked him and received information on Bozzano most people didn't know. In return she fed him information on City Council meetings citizens had never heard about. The knowledge gave Bozzano an early investment or happenings in the city that gave him an edge. Big Sally showed loyalty with his boss—an added value, when working for a powerful crime boss. That devotion could give you a pass if you ever screwed up.

"Sally?" Lucy placed the fruit back. "I need to see the man."

Sally shook his head, "Lucy, you know the rules. He doesn't like pop-ins."

"This was just put on my plate. I need to see him—now."

After doing his best, Big Sally caved to her big flashing

eyelashes as he always did. After disappearing for a minute or two, Sally returned and gave a head nod for Lucy to follow him. She walked through the mural doorway draped with a grapevine overhead.

Nothing changed in the wealthy boss man's office. It was a small space with makeshift furniture. A ray of sunlight came through the window, exposing thick dust on the windowsill.

She knew the drill. Don't sit until told or motioned to do so.

"Mr. Bozzano, good morning, and thank you for seeing me."

"What brings you here this morning, Ms. Lucy."

No pleasantries? How are you, Lucy? You look beautiful as ever. His usual bullshit opening lines ran through her mind.

She hesitated to answer, mulling over a better opening line than the nightmare story used on Rosa—which backfired.

When meeting with Bozzano, you had to be alert. He'd pick up if you were you snooping, but she was a con, and meddling was her specialty. Her eyes panned the room and locked on a picture frame at the corner of his desk. One picture frame a month ago, now two. The little things were what you watched for, as her thief of a father taught her. Lucy picked up a name written on a yellow tablet on Bozzano's desk during her last visit. He turned, and Lucy got a good look at Jay Williams, written with a checkmark next to his name. It meant nothing. Until Jay Williams's name showed up on the front page of the local *Times Picayune* newspaper. A hit-and-run driver killed him. It would have been a coincidence if she'd seen the name written other than in Bozzano's office. There was no doubt in Lucy's mind it was a hit list.

Bozzano finally motioned for her to sit. The chair was dusty, but her black leather pants could resist just about anything.

She made another attempt to look at who was in the second picture with prime placement next to the phone, and she needed a better angle.

Bozzano distracted her. "Again, why are you here?"

"Do you believe in premonitions?" She quickly shot back.

"You mean Voodoo?" Bozzano made a face. "I don't believe that bullshit."

Lucy leaned forward. "No! Truly a premonition. A strong feeling that something unpleasant is about to happen."

"No, not really," Bozzano said, then broke a grin from ear to ear. "Sometimes I think someone will die, and it happens." He paused and looked at Big Sally standing post at the entrance. "But that is usually because I ordered the person dead." He and Sally enjoyed a good laugh. "You are wasting my time. Sally, show her out."

Lucy's mind raced, and out of the blue, she shouted. "I think someone is going to kill Felipe." Her eyes locked on Bozzano, and his reaction would tell if Lucy's nightmare was correct.

Bozzano shifted in his seat, his eyes looking down. It was like playing poker, and Lucy read him like a pro.

That bastard has a hit out on Felipe.

"Why is that my problem," he said after composing himself. "You're the one that will lose revenue if he's out of the picture." Then he let out a belly laugh that vibrated the floor. "Have a good day, Lucy. Get out!"

The nightmare was confirmed when Bozzano showed his anger. He had partnered with Juan Vargas to take over Felipe's operation and leave him dead.

Lucy stood and offered a smile and a handshake across the desk. Bozzano extended his hand. Lucy shook and got a good look at the picture. *Bozzano, his wife, and a young girl in a white dress.*

She left the room under Sally's direction to the car. "By the way, Sally..." Lucy stroked his arm, then offered up a few blinks of her lashes. "Who was the little girl in the picture with Tony and his wife?"

"Annamaria, his granddaughter," he smiled. "They call her Anna. A sweet girl."

"The white dress and flowers around her head?" Lucy questioned. It looked like a celebration, so she dug deeper.

Sally gave it up quickly. "It was her First Communion. The Bozzano Family are Catholics."

Lucy let off a pleasant smile. "Cute girl." Then she kissed his cheek. "Nice seeing you, Sally."

Darby drove off and was directed to put churches in the GPS. She didn't question and found two nearby Catholic Churches, one on Tulane Avenue and another on Canal Street.

They did a drive-by, at the church on Tulane Avenue, and then stopped. "What am I looking for?" Darby asked, her head slightly turned to the back seat.

"Not sure," Lucy said. "Head over to the other church."

Darby's cell phone rang on the way to Canal Street, and

she answered, then relaying the message to Lucy. "John said he has that information for you."

Lucy didn't say a word and nodded her head back to Darby in acknowledgment. They arrived at the church on Canal Street, and Lucy pulled the window down for a better view.

"This is the church I saw in the picture on Bozzano's desk."

"Why is this important?" Darby asked but got no reply.

Lucy's mind was on lockdown, directing Darby by pointing to the corner. When making the turn, the SUV drove slowly past a schoolyard.

"About what I expected," Lucy said.

Darby glanced into the mirror. "Expected?"

"I'm not sure. But it's good to know Bozzano's granddaughter's name, and she goes to Saint Anthony's school."

CHAPTER 7

VISITORS MUST BE APPROVED by the warden in a Louisiana prison. An inmate is allowed up to ten visitors, and each can visit the inmate twice a month. Most never have that many, but Felipe needed all ten slots and would take more if he could. His drug business and contact with the cartel didn't miss a beat. Visitors at this prison were allowed on Wednesdays and Sundays in a large room overseen by guards, microphones, and cameras.

Lucy needed to get in that prison to visit Felipe—and quick. Every second he was in there his life was in danger. She did what was necessary and had to find someone who owed her a favor.

Just before noon, Darby dropped Lucy at the Burdette House. Wanda, her mother, who ran the house, had a private office away from any residents. It was the best place to make a confidential call other than from the back seat of the SUV. Le Salon had too many nosey women walking around, and the City Council office was out of the question. Operators could listen in at will.

Lucy's top two security men had left to run a food

truck with her backing. It was an excellent cash business that allowed her to funnel more of Felipe's drug money into usable cash. They recommended a man for the head of security. He stepped in and never missed a beat in keeping the Burdette House and Wally's Manor safe for the battered women and men.

Darby headed to the kitchen where she usually hung out while Lucy conducted business in the management office. Lucy stood in the doorway and shot Wanda a look, sitting behind a desk, and it was the clue to gather her things and get out.

Wanda grabbed her day planner and, in passing, brushed Lucy's face. "Nice to see you, honey." Like any mother, she noticed her daughter was drained. "You're okay? You're looking tired."

"I'm good. It's been a rough morning," Lucy said, rolling her eyes.

"You need to take time off. Rent a beach house and sit out in the sand—just do nothing for a few days," Wanda said gathering her things.

"That would be nice. But I don't have time right now—soon though," Lucy said giving Wanda a peck on the cheek when she left.

She flopped in the desk chair and flipped through her black book, which kept the names of people who owed her a favor. She donated to political campaigns and did favors for French Quarter merchants. She turned pages looking for the one person who could best help her.

A knock came at the door, and a lady from the kitchen brought in a tray carrying a an assortment of teas and a pot

NIGHT TERRORS

of hot water. She gave Lucy a smile and placed the tray on the desk.

"Mrs. Wanda said, you might like some tea," she said then closed the door behind her.

Lucy looked over names and then poured some tea. "Yep, it's time to call Thomas Trahan the Governor." She scrolled her address book and called the governor's cell phone, but he didn't answer. She waited, and he sometimes called back, but after five minutes, she gave up. Next was a call to Mayor Sam Algarotti, and he picked up on the second ring.

"Lucy? Can I call you back?" He spoke softly. "I am in the middle of something at the governor's mansion."

Sam, a longtime client of Club Twilight and Thomas, should have been charged with voter fraud for what he had asked of her during their campaigns. Lucy owned both and could demand just about anything.

"Any other people with you two?

Sam hesitated but did reply with a yes.

"Sorry to interrupt but put him on the phone."

In a whisper, he replied. "That's not a good idea."

"Put him on," she insisted.

The phone went silent, but not for long. "Lucy, I was about to call you back," Thomas said with a muffled sound. He had moved into a smaller room away from his guest.

Lucy rolled her eyes. *You lying bastard. You probably soil your pants every time you hear I'm calling.*

"I need a favor and quick."

Thomas tried to brush her off. "Not a problem. But like I said, I am in the middle of a meeting."

Lucy bypassed his suggestion and asked anyway. "I need you to contact the warden at the Winnfield Prison and get me on the visitor's list for Felipe Cruz."

There was a long hesitation. "Dammit Lucy, you interrupted me for this drug-pushing clown?" He often had an attitude, and it showed this time. "Call the prison in a few days, and I'll get your name on the list."

In a convincing tone, Lucy replied, "No! You call me in ten minutes with the okay. I don't call in favors too often. This I need, and now."

Thomas pushed back, but Lucy cut him off.

"Your reputation and an investigation into how you handle your campaign fund rely on your quick response."

"You're threatening me?"

"Nine minutes left." She disconnected the call as Thomas talked.

Sipping her tea, she leaned back into the desk chair. Her eyes shifted the room. *Maybe it wasn't the time to push Thomas so hard.* As usual, she was second-guessing herself.

She called down to the kitchen and found Darby having lunch but mostly romancing the lady workers in the kitchen.

"Yeah, boss?" Darby said, taking the call on the second ring.

"Put Winnfield Prison in your GPS and tell me how long of a drive."

"Unfortunately, no need to," she said. "Been there a few times. It's my cousin's residence for the last five years."

"How long of a drive from New Orleans?"

"Three hours." Darby snapped back.

"But, without getting a ticket or going to jail for speeding excessively?"

She laughed. "You're no fun, Boss. Three and a half hours."

Lucy's cell phone rang. The screen showed an unknown number was calling. She answered.

"Lucinda Jones?" A pleasant woman's voice announced.

"Yes."

"Please hold for Warden Sheldon LeBlanc," the person said.

"Hello, Ms. Jones?" A deep southern drawl voice said. "I'm Warden LeBlanc. I understand you want to visit Felipe Cruz."

"Yes, sir."

"When is your visit?"

Lucy took a deep breath. She didn't weigh her words. "I'll be there in under four hours." His response time was quick. "Not a problem. Bring identification," the warden said. "And Ms. Jones. Write my number down. If you need anything, call me direct. Any friend of the governor is a friend of mine."

She wrote his phone number down. "Thank you."

Lucy hung up and sent a courtesy text thanking the governor. She received a quick reply.

"Happy to help. Are we good?"

The text brought a smile to her face. *Are we good?* It was a giveaway that she still controlled the governor. She answered him with a text. "We're terrific, my friend."

CHAPTER 8

DARBY ROLLED THE SUV into the prison visitor's lot in record time from New Orleans. When checking their speed on the drive up, Darby gave a few glances to the back seat, but Lucy was too buried in her phone to notice how fast they traveled.

A half-full parking lot showed few visitors. As a teenager, the prison where Lucy visited her father was packed from open to close.

They followed the signs and came around the building to the first security point. From what Lucy remembered, there would be several checkpoints before coming face to face with the prisoner. It was all too familiar and brought back unpleasant memories when visiting her father, Edgar, in prison. They all had the same cold, scary feeling upon approach.

"Name and identification," the first guard said.

It was what Lucy expected from a prison guard with an attitude, and she never met one that didn't appear to hate their job. She pulled out her driver's license, which she had ready, and handed it to him.

"Lucinda Jones," he read from the license out loud. "Who are you here to visit?"

"Felipe Cruz," she answered. She knew the game. Play nice, or the guard will give you a hard time, and you'll be detained unnecessarily—or look over the visitor's log a few times like he doesn't see your name, forcing you to wait. Sometimes it would be for as long as an hour which cut into your visiting time. She remembered it happened once visiting her father. He told her the reasoning for the issue was that the guards hated him. Lucy knew better because sometimes she'd catch a ride to the jail only to sit outside. Edgar's privileges were taken away the night before for speaking out to a guard.

She studied the guard's name tag attached to his shirt pocket. "Clay? That must be an old family name?"

He ignored her question.

"You're here to see Felipe Cruz?" His head cocked to the side, and his eyes widened as he showed off his pearly white teeth.

Lucy gave a head nod and smiled back. Her eyes shifted to Darby.

"What the hell?" Darby whispered.

At first, Lucy thought he was flirting. She read up on the dress code and ensured she complied. No low-cut tops or skin-tight clothing, no heels, and only rubber-soled shoes.

The guard slightly pulled Lucy's arm, moved her to the side, and smiled again. He said something into the radio attached to his shirt near his shoulder, but she couldn't make out what was said.

"Roger that," was the reply.

She handed Darby her purse and kept her driver's license.

"I'll wait in the car," Darby said.

"You are welcome to sit in the guard's lounge," Clay said. His eyes shifted Darby's way.

Again, Lucy's looked at Darby, and both lipped: W*hat the hell.*

"No, thank you," she gave a wink of her eye his way. "This place gives me the creeps." With Lucy's purse in hand, she hurried back to the car.

She addressed Clay. "What's going on?"

"Just sit tight." He said and stood with her while someone else took over his spot at the checkpoint.

"Yes, sir?" an approaching guard announced.

"We'll escort Ms. Jones to the private guest room," he said. "And Ms. Jones, I am named after my grandfather, Clay Morrow."

"Well, it's a beautiful name," Lucy said and followed the guard.

Guest room? Ran through her mind the entire walk. *She'd never heard anything so formal referred to in prison.*

They passed a large open room with inmates sitting with family members. Bypassing the area, they continued walking, and Clay stopped at a solid closed door. He gave a head gesture to a guard standing post. When the door opened, Felipe sat at a table facing the entrance in the center of the room.

"You know the agreement," Clay said. "The door stays open."

Felipe gave a grin. Lucy had seen the grin often. "Not a problem. Can you stay long enough for me to get a hug?"

NIGHT TERRORS

Clay rolled his eyes to the guard, and he turned away. "Hurry it up."

Felipe gave Lucy a hug and a kiss on the cheek. "What brings you here, Mama?" They hugged it out until Clay cut them off. They took seats at the table, and Clay left the room. Lucy spoke, and Felipe ran his finger across his lip. Then he motioned to the guard.

The guard looked down the hallway on both sides and slowly closed the door.

"Now you can speak," Felipe said, pointing to the room's four corners. "The cameras are focused on the center of the table, so the monitors cannot pick up the closed door. The guard who is on my payroll guaranteed the microphones are off."

Lucy scanned the room, looking for a surveillance device, even the smallest button by the light switch, fixture, or along the baseboard. "That had to cost."

"How else can I spend my money?" Felipe patted her hand from across the table. "How are you? I hear big things are happening, Councilwoman."

Lucy would say nothing that might incriminate herself. She didn't care how much Felipe paid out to guards—she didn't trust them. She'd heard too many tales from her father about how he paid them only to have one turn on him and get him placed in the "hole" for a week.

"Felipe, I am concerned with your safety," she whispered.

"Mama? What are you whispering about?"

"Dammit, Felipe." She said, slamming the table with

the palm of her hand. "My night terrors are back—you were killed."

"In here? No way," Felipe laughed." Too much money is spread around to guards and their wives. Clay is the kingpin, so I paid his children's school for the year, and I even promised I'd continue paying for eighteen months after I am out."

Lucy sat at an angle for a view of the door. "What if someone else paid more?"

Felipe's eyes shifted much like he did when considering handling a situation. "No, too many people are paid off for one to break the chain," he shook his head. "Why are you coming to me with this?"

She rolled her eyes at him. "Hello—I am protecting my investment. Remember who I am? Without me, your clean money comes to a crashing halt."

"Lucy, didn't you have a nightmare about me once before?" He stood and walked a circle. "I am still here."

"Yeah, but your cousin is not. He went to the meeting you were supposed to join." Lucy stood and grabbed him by the shoulders. "I told you I got a tip that it was a police sting, but I made it up. It was a dream. Your cousin showed up in the same type of black SUV you're chauffeured around. He and the driver were shredded with bullets before they got out of the car." She pushed him back. "I had a nightmare three nights earlier you were gunned down."

They took a seat and calmed down. There was a knock at the door, and it opened. A prisoner came in with two coffees.

"What is this? The concierge level?" She laughed

and took the coffee, and the inmate left, closing the door behind her.

She went over the dream with Felipe to the best she could remember.

"Juan Vargas?" Felipe questioned.

Lucy dug deep into what she experienced as if it happened. Vargas and Bozzano were partnering up, and the first order of business was to cut the head off the snake. It popped into her head, and she didn't remember the man who had assaulted her that night in her dream saying it until now.

"He said to cut the head off the snake?" Felipe said it with concern.

Lucy nodded. "Best that I recall."

Back to wandering the room, but this time out of concern, Felipe circled the table and came up behind Lucy. "That's a term the Colombians use when they take over a territory. Did he say those precise words?"

"Yes!" Lucy shouted, "The best I remember."

The door popped open, and the guard looked in. "Everything okay?"

"Sorry, we're fine," Lucy said, shooting the guard a side glance.

Lucy sat staring at the wall, surprised Felipe was taking everything seriously. He was the guy who thought he was invincible. Always speaking out, no one could get to him. He once told Lucy to watch her back in his business. There was always some young punk coming up through the ranks who wanted to step in your shoes. Juan Vargas fit that description. Meeting him in Miami years ago, Juan was only a teenager looking to make a fast buck. Now he wanted to take over Felipe's business.

Her eyes followed Felipe the best she could while he paced the room, talking to himself, walking in circles around the table to the point it made her dizzy. She now knew this was a mistake ever telling him, and maybe the nightmare was just that—a bad dream.

There was a knock at the door, and the guard put his head in. "Five minutes."

"Guard," Felipe shouted.

The man opened the door further and stepped in. "Yes?"

"I'll tell you when my time is up, understand?"

Lucy worked Felipe to a boiling point. The veins in his bugging eyes gave off a red glow. She experienced his rage a few times, and it would intensify if he wasn't talked down.

"Look, Felipe, I can only tell you I had the dream, and after hearing Bozzano beat around the bush when I picked his brain—well." She paused. "The bastard is involved."

"If I had to guest, Bozzano or his men would never be close to the drugs. He's the money man."

Lucy hesitated to mention the part in her dream where the man threatened her if she stopped washing the drug money. *It's the same job…with a new boss and a cheaper rate.* He said it like she was applying for a job and negotiating a salary. But she had no say. He clarified that she'd continue to wash Vargas's money, or she'd die.

She should have known Felipe would quickly figure it out—and he did. Taking a seat, he pulled her arms across the table. His nostrils flared, and the veins in his eyes thickened. "I guess Vargas wants you to wash his money."

Lucy's insides shook. She was now questioning what she had done. *Maybe I read the dream wrong? Perhaps I should have left it alone and would see how it all worked out.* The thought ran through her mind as she wondered how to answer him.

She broke the silence. "Yes. Vargas expects me to work for him and Bozzano."

"You think you can waltz your candy ass from Tupelo to my town? I trained you as a pup, and you were wet behind the ears. And now you think you can walk away? Not going to happen!"

Lucy let him ramble. It wasn't the way it went down, and she was far from wet behind the ears when she rolled into the French Quarter. Taking what she learned from her crook of a father running cons for years, she added Vivian's criminal mind to her resume. She showed Felipe how to wash his money and put it into play so he could invest.

The door opened, and the guard stepped in, but Felipe shouted before he could open his mouth.

"You come in again, I'll rip your arm off and jam it down your throat."

"Clay is coming down the hall," the guard said in a shaky voice.

"Felipe, take the information for what it is worth. If you walk out of here, Bozzano might hunt you down, and if you stay in jail, he'll have you shanked in the shower when you least expect." Lucy walked to the door and stopped. "It was my night terrors working overtime, and maybe nonsense, but in my mind, it's real. I did my part and alerted you. If it were me—I'd watch my back."

ౚ

They drove back to New Orleans, and on their way Darby kept silent. Lucy sat in the back seat, dismal as her nerves were on edge. Prisons made her uneasy and battling with Felipe added to the drama of her complex life. She took a deep breath and then exhaled, doing her best to follow her doctor's advice on how to shake anxiety, but her mind was too deep into the meeting. It just didn't go as she planned. Anticipating Felipe to show some appreciation for her coming forward backfired on her.

"I did the right thing in telling Felipe, correct Darby?"

The rearview mirror positioned on Lucy's face gave Darby a look at a woman second-guessing herself. "Not to add to your stress, Boss, but the cow is out of the barn."

"Yeah, I know it's too late. But what if I am wrong? I could start a blood bath."

"What if you didn't tell Felipe, and he was gunned down on the street? How would you feel? Would you be concerned you lost a friend or millions of dollars a year in washing his money?"

Lucy looked at the mirror and locked eyes with Darby. "The rage Felipe showed me today reminded me he has no loyalty, feeling, or regard for anyone's life. He will cut you out of his life the second he has no use for you. And what I mean is when he has no use for you, he'll chop you in pieces, put you in a sack, and feed you to the alligators in the swamp."

NIGHT TERRORS

There was a pause. Darby's eyes shifted from the back seat to the road. With a cock to her head, she replied. "Then I guess you made the right decision. You told him to watch his back—and you watch yours too."

A buzzing sound came from Lucy's purse. Her phone was placed on vibrate after handing the bag off to Darby at the prison. No name on the screen only meant the person wasn't in her address book, and she didn't answer unless she knew who was calling.

Quickly following was a text with pictures on the screen. The message read: *My daughter Jane and her friend Beth Wiggins. They are in the room with the firearms.*

She read the text to Darby, saying it was from John. The pictures showed Beth holding a machine gun. Lucy passed the phone to Darby. She pulled to the side of the road and thumbed through the pictures.

"Lucy? This is a dangerous arms dealer. Do you see the stacks of crates behind them? That could be hundreds of guns. Those kids are at risk if Beth's father finds out. With pictures? They're dead."

"What kind of guns are those?"

Darby handed the phone back. "The kind every terrorist wants." She glanced into the mirror and got a look at Lucy. "How do you get involved with these people?"

The car went silent. Lucy stared down at the pictures, then with a slow rise of her eyes, she replied. "I don't know. Somehow, I'll sort it out."

Before she texted John back, another message came through from him. *My daughter Jane did her part and got Beth*

Wiggins to show the weapons again. Please help before something terrible happens.

Lucy turned the phone off and dropped it in her purse.

CHAPTER 9

ON HIGHWAY 425 JUST south of New Iberia, a flat-bed trailer loaded with lumber slowed down and turned down a gravel road. It was identified by a bright yellow sign stating *private property* with a camera mounted on the top. The driver pulled forward to a gate, allowing the truck following them to pull off the highway.

The flat-bed driver got out and pressed the button on the call box, and someone answered immediately. The man was told to stand away and look up at the camera, and he did. A bright flash all but blinded him even though it was daylight.

Security was tight. *Who the hell lives here? Some Cartel drug dealer?* The driver mumbled, getting back in the truck.

"I heard the owner is more feared than any cartel," the passenger said, shooting his partner with a crazy-eyed stare. "I heard this is a hunting lodge for a Federal Judge, and he's the guy that puts drug dealers behind bars."

The trucks pulled through the gates, and they quickly closed behind them. They made it around a blacktop road for about one hundred yards and came to a guardhouse. The man with a weapon strapped to his side waved them through.

A construction crew was waiting, and the load was transferred to the ground. Appliances and cabinets rolled into a garage for an outdoor kitchen.

They finished, and the truck's driver said, "Let's check out the river in the back."

"No! Let's get the hell out of here," his partner replied. "Anyplace that needs this much protection—I don't want to be around longer than necessary."

***

A black town car pulled to the curb on Tulane Avenue in front of the New Orleans Criminal Court Building. Douglas Zimmerman sat in the back seat and waited for his driver to open the door. Douglas stood curbside while the driver reached in for his coat and helped slip the custom-made jacket on, much like he was in a fancy men's clothing store. Then he ran his hand across the back collar, smoothing it out and ensuring it was lint-free.

Douglas Zimmerman was known around town as the "Dapper Duke." He was always dressed fashionably by a renowned tailor on Fifth Avenue in New York. Highly paid, he always got the job done by either winning the case or pleading the charges down to a lesser charge and a reduced sentence.

This was someone Felipe wished he'd hired early on when he was arrested. It took four years to undo his first attorney's damage. Having a prosecutor get leverage in the courtroom was something Douglas never allowed.

Douglas climbed the concrete steps leading to the federal court entrance. Inside he faced security and was hand scanned with an electronic device. Then for added protection, he emptied the contents of his pockets into a basket and walked through a scanner.

"Good morning Mr. Zimmerman. Where are you heading?" the guard asked.

"Judge Elton Bordelon," he replied, picking up his items from the basket.

He acknowledged the receptionist when he stepped into Judge Bordelon's office and made his meaningless small talk with the secretary. He would take a seat and was prepared to wait. An appointment didn't guarantee a face-to-face meeting with the judge when he arrived. No matter what was on the judge's agenda, appointments and court could be delayed when another case needed immediate attention.

This time he was lucky, and shortly after taking a seat, the receptionist's phone rang.

"Judge Bordelon will see you now," she said and directed Douglas into the judge's chamber.

"Good morning, your honor," Douglas said, sitting in an overstuffed leather chair in front of a massive wood desk.

The judge gave a smirk and pressed a button on his phone. A man in a suit appeared seconds later, and Douglas knew him as a security team member. A hand motion from the judge and the man knew what to do. So did Douglas, and he stood, taking his coat off and lifting his arms.

The guard checked him closely, running his hands up Douglas's legs and way higher than expected.

"Watch your hands, big fellow. This is our first date…" They both laughed.

"He's clean, Your Honor," the guard said, then exited the chamber.

Douglas sat in the leather chair, facing the desk. "Really, judge? You think I'm coming in here with a wire?"

"Doug, you know why I've been a judge for twenty-eight years?"

The high-powered attorney hated such an informal name, especially since only his mother still called him by his childhood nickname. The judge used it to make him angry.

"No, judge, but please tell me."

"I am cautious, Doug." He smiled. "Now, we can talk freely."

The judge walked around the desk, resting on the front edge. "I got a call," he said, then paused as he smiled. "A load of lumber and cooking equipment was delivered to my country house.

Country house? More like a compound... ran through Douglas's mind.

"Is that so, sir."

"Yep, top-line equipment just like my wife wanted."

Knowing Doug was clean, he still talked vaguely. "Not sure what it all cost, but it should turn out nice."

I'll tell you. A hundred and twenty-six thousand dollars. Douglas played the game and just let it all run around in his head. *A drop in the bucket to get out of jail on a technicality.*

"So, what are you here for, Doug?" Elton never let his guard down in making Douglas say why he wanted an appointment.

"That Felipe Cruz case?"

"Why are you taking up my time with this crap?" Judge Bordelon said and stepped behind his desk.

"Excuse me, your honor?" Douglas stood, hands resting on the desk. "What's going on?"

"Got you sweating, Doug? Did your stomach make a few flips?"

He was a tough attorney and could stand up to the best prosecutors and even a judge, But this made him nervous.

"Get out of here," the judge said, stopping Doug at the door. "Felipe was released an hour ago."

"Then why all the bullshit!"

"Because I enjoy watching you sweat." Judge Bordelon smiled. "And Doug, I agree with your findings. I'm sending the District Attorney a letter on how his incompetent staff screwed up the case by putting a drug dealer back on the street."

"What about the Feds?" Douglas asked.

"Oh, don't worry, the FBI director in New Orleans will get an earful from the district senator." Judge Bordelon gave a loud gut laugh. "Congratulations, Doug! You got a criminal out of jail and a federal prosecutor no doubt knocked down to working nights in surveillance.

CHAPTER 10

AT 3:22 P.M., THE prison warden signed off on Felipe Cruz's release order, and shortly after, he walked out a free man.

A jacked-up white Jeep with twenty-two-inch chrome rims sat outside the prison walls waiting for Felipe. A backup black SUV with heavily tinted glass waited behind the Jeep.

Two men dressed in suits sat in a dark sedan parked thirty yards away, not caring if they were seen, watching the two vehicles through binoculars.

"How did the prosecutors mess this up?" The FBI agent with the binoculars asked his partner.

He quickly shot back, "We should go harass them. I'm sure they have tons of illegal guns in the lead car."

"No," the driver said. "We are going to build a solid case this time. Charges that some fancy attorney can't pick apart."

The massive iron gates opened, and Felipe Cruz stood by Clay's side. Instructed not to move until Clay gave the order, Felipe obeyed.

The gates moved slowly, and Clay chatted in a way the

tower and cameras couldn't see him. "Felipe, I did my part, and you have been safe. Make sure you keep your end of the bargain."

Felipe didn't look his way and answered. "Clay, I am a man of my word. Your children's school will continue to get the tuition. I probably overpaid because I was never really in danger. Who has the balls to try and take me out?"

"Felipe Cruz, step forward," an armed guard in the tower shouted over a microphone when the gate opened.

"Thanks for nothing, asshole," Felipe said, looking back at Clay. He then stepped over the line between imprisonment and the free world.

He walked about four steps when Clay shouted. "You were ordered dead. I stepped in and shut it down."

Felipe's face wrinkled, "What? No way." He showed worry.

"That's why your privileges were taken away a few days ago. Confined to your cell unless one of my guards moved you. It was for your own protection until I could get a handle on the attempted hit."

"Who ordered me dead?" He yelled. The veins in his neck thickened.

"I don't know. I got wind of it from a lifer and shut it down."

"Who ordered it? Who!"

The sound of the iron gates closed, and the grinding gears of automatic locks could be heard as they tightened. That quick Felipe was on the outside, and the celebration began. He was not in the party mood but mustered up a fake smile shaking hands with his crew. Then Rosa locked eyes with him, and they kissed. Grabbing her waist, he spun her around. The hugs and shouting went on way longer than anyone leaving prison. It was all planned just to piss the guards off. It was something Felipe told his crew he wanted if he ever got out. They came through with his wishes, and the guards in the tower turned their backs.

"That's okay, turn your backs," Felipe shouted. "You can't turn your ears off." Laughter echoed off the prison walls.

"Go ahead and celebrate," the agent in the car said. "You'll slip up, and this time, you will not walk out of jail."

The dust kicked up as the Jeep and the black SUV passed the sedan on the side of the road. As the vehicles passed, Felipe's crew waved to the agents, shouting something in Spanish.

"Do you know what they said?" The agent behind the wheel asked.

His partner shook his head, "no."

"I'm sure they didn't say. Have a nice day."

The cars coasted into the neighborhood with the horns blowing. People stood on porches waving Felipe home. The boomboxes positioned on the front steps were cranked up, blasting Spanish Music down the street.

Felipe was on his home turf, and he exited the car without concern. No one could get past the corners without being gunned down. He waved to his people.

The houses that lined the street were all owned by Felipe thanks to Lucy for washing his money and her creative accounting. He vetted the resident himself and trusted people, like uncles, cousins, and friends, who were placed in the houses. They were given living quarters, groceries, and cash to sit on their porch and watch for the police or other gangs.

Felipe gave one last wave to the neighbors then pulled his wife closer, and his party planner escorted the couple followed by his crew.

The courtyard that Felipe copied from a hotel on Royal Street was as he remembered. Palm trees and colorful seasonal flowers lined the walkway with the fire pit in the center. A pig had been roasting over a slow flame since early that morning. When greeting guests, Felipe and Rosa sat on oversized chairs like a king and queen.

The music got louder, and the bar opened. Two men paraded around the courtyard with a magnum of Dom Perignon champagne, a sword, and crystal flutes on a wood board held chest high. The wood board was placed at Felipe's feet.

The music stopped, and the guest stood silent as the head wine master from a local store where Felipe ordered cases at a time presented the champagne.

He bowed his head with the bottle in one hand and the sword in the other. "Welcome home, Felipe." With one swift, forceful move, the blade slid against the neck of the bottle, popping the cork into the air. The music cranked louder, and champagne was served.

One of the crew members whispered in Felipe's ear.

He quickly shook his head. "Sí."

At the doorway between the house and the courtyard stood Douglas Zimmerman. He walked with two of the crew down the brick walkway.

With the wave of his hand, the music stopped, and Felipe stood. "Thank you, federal prosecutors, for the big screw-up!" He lifted his glass. "And thanks to the Dapper Duke, my attorney."

Douglas and Felipe hugged as the crowd clapped.

"Thank you, my brother," Felipe said. "You need anything—call me." And with a tighter grip, he pulled Douglas closer. "I mean anything!"

Pulling the attorney's hand up high, he lifted a glass of champagne. "To the Dapper Duke!"

Once again, the music blasted this time into the neighborhood. Cheers came from a distance. Felipe walked on water to the people in this small community and could do no wrong. He was their livelihood, and they would protect him to the end.

The pig was carved, and people stood in line for thick juicy slices, then moved to a buffet where all Felipe's favorite side dishes were prepared in covered bowls. The first three plates were hand-carried to Felipe, where he, Rosa, and Douglas sat at a private table.

Rosa was not sheltered with Felipe's criminal record, and Douglas talked freely of the details. There was not enough time for Felipe to deliver the money to Douglas for the final details of his release. But Felipe guaranteed him the funds would be paid in cash the next day for the construction work on Judge Bordelon's camp.

There were no issues or red flags on Douglas Zimmerman's bank account for accepting large amounts of cash for payment. Who would take a check from a criminal for any amount? He was known as the attorney for criminals and demanded payment in cash. How his clients got the money was not his concern, and it was up to law enforcement to pursue that avenue if they thought they could win.

The three ate and continued to drink. Felipe checked his watch and motioned to his number one man to come forward.

"Are they in position?" He asked.

The man nodded his head. "Waiting for the okay."

"Do it and lean hard," Felipe said.

Douglas's eyes shifted from Felipe to the man. "Is there something I should know about?"

"No, just some unfinished prison business. Drink up!" Felipe shouted, lifting his champagne.

CHAPTER 11

THE CALL CAME THROUGH, and one man answered. He didn't talk but listened. The voice on the other end said: *It's a go.* That was all he needed to hear, and he clicked his cellphone off.

Two tall men neatly dressed in button-down shirts, starched jeans with a firm crease, and fancy Ostrich leather booths stepped out of a Porsche Cayenne Turbo. They were not twins but brothers two years apart and looked alike. They were so close in size and looks, their mother named them Mark and Clark and dressed them the same.

They were highly paid drug runners for Felipe and didn't fall into the stereotype the police profiled. These two educated white men were clean-cut, had no record, and had a luxury vehicle that could outrun and even crush a police roadblock—if necessary. Most of all, they had connections.

Felipe once provided Mark and Clark with the description of a woman he saw in the prison visitor's room. He called her "Plain Jane," and she could fly under the prison radar on visiting day. They found the homely-looking woman in two days with only a shirt brand, color, and a local merchant bag logo to go on. For the right cash, she was on Felipe's payroll and moving drugs in prison on visiting day. Drugs and payment were given the night before, and she had to get creative on how to get them inside the jail. The two men were Felipe's go-to for the challenging assignments.

They walked in unison through the parking lot to the entrance identified by a sign with a single lightbulb shining on the name—The Hole.

After retirement, a bar was started by two prison guards famous for putting inmates in solitary confinement, known to prisoners as the "hole." It became a shift hangout for the guards and prison workers—a place to unwind before going home after a stressful day of dealing with the lower than low, discussing people of the world. At least that's what they told their wives, and it was the reason they came home smashed most nights after work.

Felipe often pumped Clay about his life after his shift. A simple question addressed to Clay he looked tired, and Felipe got an earful. He didn't open up fully at first. Still, once learning Clay struggled with his kid's tuition, Felipe saw the opportunity and acted quickly. Soon a cash payment arrived at the school, pre-paying both of his children's tuition for the year. From that point on, Felipe owned Clay, and all his demands were met.

Clay became a motor-mouth saying one day: *All I want to do is get over to the Hole and get a cold one.* Then he spilled the history of the place, how often the workers stopped in, and how he could walk home if he was too drunk to drive, which he had done a few times.

Mark held the door open for Clark, and they stepped into the bar. The few people inside noticed them as if they had two heads and an eye on their forehead.

"Can I help you?" the bartender asked, giving them the once over.

"Just a couple cold ones," Mark said as they took a seat.

"Passing through?" The ex-prison worker-turned-bar-owner asked.

Mark smiled. "Visiting my Dad at the prison."

Always skeptical of non-locals, these two all but had "tourist" written across their faces. The bartender dropped two frosty glasses of tap beer in front. "Visiting hours closed a few hours ago. Why are you still in these parts?"

It wasn't Mark's first rodeo, and he shot back the correct answer. "Well, we would have been home hours ago." He pushed Clark on the shoulder. "If my dumb brother could read the highway signs."

"Hell, the signs are confusing. All I did was go in a big loop," he laughed. "And we're back in the same place we left—an hour ago."

The bartender bent over the bar and motioned. "Out the parking lot, turn left. Take a right at Highway 92, and about three miles down, you'll hit the interstate."

"It was that simple, dumbass," Mark said, again giving Clark a push.

"Doesn't matter if you're going east or west," the bartender patted the bar. "Let me know if you need anything else."

Clark shifted his eye to his brother. "Are we that obvious?"

"Looking at these shit-kickers, they seldom see people with clean clothes," he replied.

They spotted Clay alone at a table. Felipe's description described him perfectly, and there was no doubt since his name tag was still attached to his shirt. Mark couldn't make it out for sure from a distance but would confirm as he got closer. From the looks of things, he was on his way to getting lit with three empties on the table.

Clark took his beer and walked towards Clay's table, and Mark followed. Making eye contact with three men shooting pool, they gave a smile and a friendly gesture their way. The bartender was preoccupied with a lady who appeared to have had a few too many.

Mark put his beer on Clay's table and took a seat quickly. Clark hugged the wall behind Clay and sipped his beer.

"How are you, my friend?" Mark asked. Then checked his name tag. "You're Clay, right?"

He flipped his ID badge with two fingers, "It does not take a genius to figure that out. Do I know you?" Clay shot back.

Mark pulled a handgun from his belt and planted it in Clay's stomach under the table. Clay's eyes widened, and he reacted.

"Let's not get excited. No need to have your guts sprayed on the pool table felt."

Clark patted Clay's shoulder as a man passed, heading to the bathroom door like they were old friends.

Mark got to the point. "Everything is cool, and no one will get hurt. Just need to know who came to you with the hit on Felipe?"

He jerked his head to look over his shoulder. "Felipe is out of jail a half a day, and he pulls this—? I'll have him back in jail by tomorrow morning."

Mark smiled. "Now lower your voice." Then he pushed the gun between Clay's legs. "Don't be the asshole we all know you can be. The smart thing to do is give up a name."

Luckily, someone dropped money in the jukebox, and some country song crying about somebody doing someone wrong came on. It was just the distraction and buffer they needed.

One more push of the gun between Clay's legs. "A name," he said.

"A prisoner came to me, and he might have made the story up just to get some privileges," Clay said, his eyes showing concern.

"I'm getting hungry," Clark said. "Screw this guy. Just shoot him."

Mark shook his head. "You see, Clay, my brother is impatient. Give it up, or we'll leave a lot of bodies behind." He pushed the gun deeper into Clay.

"Okay! All I know is a visitor would deliver fifty grand to an inmate's family when Felipe goes down."

"Give the name up!" Mark demanded.

"I checked the visiting log, and the guy's name was Salvador Ricci," Clay said. "He visited that day with inmate Dominick Ricci, and I think it's his brother or maybe a cousin."

Clay gave up what Mark thought was all he knew. He warned that his girl's school tuition would end if he talked of their visit.

NIGHT TERRORS

"Sara and Mary—they're your children's names?"

Clay showed no emotion. His head moved like a robot, moving up and down. "How did you know?"

Mark smiled. "It doesn't matter. You open your mouth, and they will disappear one day walking home from school."

He assured Clay they had scouted the school and his kid's pattern from when they left school and walked home. It even included their visit a few times a week at the ice cream parlor on Main Street.

Clay's eyes widened, and fear took over. He had dealt with the hardest of criminals, letting none into his personal life. He couldn't believe Felipe worked his way over a few short years. Now he had no choice but to comply with demands.

Clark got the bartender's attention, dropped a twenty, and returned with three long-neck Dixie Beers.

"Here you go, Clay," Clark said, placing the beers on the table. "Now you have a reason to get plastered."

The two brothers casually strolled to the front door.

"Thanks for the directions," Mark said with a hardy wave to the bartender.

They made it to the car without even a head turn from anyone. Mark cranked the Cayenne Turbo to a deep rumble and accelerated a few times shaking the old building. Then he dropped it in gear and pelted gravel before hitting the open highway.

CHAPTER 12

Mostly, New Orleans is quiet, except for sirens in the distance, like any city. They could be police, emergency units, or fire trucks blasting, and the sounds become second nature to a point where you just ignore them.

When Darby drove Lucy to City Hall, she heard the dreadful horn followed by a loud siren coming from behind. A glance into the mirror, she watched cars pull to the side of the avenue as fire trucks approached. Three trucks headed to the river, and once they passed, the traffic flowed again.

History has shown when a fire breaks out in the French Quarter or Warehouse District, the fire department overcompensates. It takes too long to get the big diesel rolling to send one unit and discover the fire is spreading among the closely built warehouses or storefronts.

"How does a metal building catch on fire?" Darby asked, watching the trucks run traffic lights on their mission

"It's the content—cotton, lumber, coffee…plus these places are over a hundred years old," Lucy said. "When built, the roof and framing were all wood supports."

NIGHT TERRORS

It was frightening to Lucy the story Vivian told salon workers every time a fire truck came down Royal Street. Her grandmother told her the French Quarter was destroyed by fire in the 1800s when she was a child.

Lucy explained how it was told to her that early firefighting equipment was nothing more than a tank of water pulled by horses.

"I've seen a small brushfire take out a barn and a supply of hay for the winter within minutes. Fire can spread fast," Darby added, parking at the side entrance of City Hall.

At the curbside, Lucy sniffed the air looking up at the smoke. Black cloud puffs turned gray. "Water is getting to the fire now." She sat on the back seat and put on a pair of slip-on rubber sole shoes.

"You're still taking the stairs?" Darby asked. "You need to come to the gym with me, and I'll give you a workout."

"No thanks, I've seen your workout," Lucy said. "I'm not looking to get crippled in the process."

Darby bid her goodbye and then looked over the list of errands Lucy passed to her on a sticky note. Standing outside the vehicle, she watched Lucy walk into the entrance of City Hall and clear security before pulling off. She was in her bodyguard mode, ensuring her number one was safe inside the building before leaving.

Inside, Lucy sidestepped the mass of people rushing through the hallways. As usual, most were late for work but still talked on cell phones while weaving between people to get to the elevators. She took the stairwell and hit the steps vigorously to the third floor.

Good job, Lucy. You made it without stopping or sounding like you smoke two packs a day… she thought to herself.

Lucy never had to worry about her figure. Darby often reminded her she didn't exercise, which would catch up with her someday.

She swapped the rubber shoes for heels in a soft bag from her oversize purse and walked to her office. A few deep breaths helped until she saw an unexpecting visitor waiting at her office door.

"What the hell, Felipe?" She said, rushing to him. Her head spun like a top, checking to see if anyone noticed them together. The council member's community secretary was just inside the front entrance and always at work on time. Lucy gave a jerk of Felipe's jacket, pulling him to her private access a few doors down.

"Sit!" She said and pointed to a chair in front of her desk. Lucy opened the door slightly and peeked out into the reception area. "Hi, good morning."

"Good morning, councilwoman," the secretary replied.

"No calls. I'll let you know when I am available." She closed and locked the door. "Felipe, you know the agreement. No visits to the salon, Burdette House, and sure the hell not at City Hall." She flopped into the desk chair and opened her purse. Out came a cell phone. "This is our only communication."

Felipe had a smirk that turned Lucy's stomach, and she only tolerated it because they were business partners. He paved the road to riches for her, so she overlooked his condescending attitude.

"All your rules went out the window with the dream

you had. No cell phone today, and I wanted to tell you in person," he said, as he pulled closer to the desk.

He detailed the night before. Shortly after Lucy left the party, Felipe and his wife stood watching the rest of his friends drive down the street. Some turned in driveways and went the opposite way. There were celebrating as they left, shouting and horns sounding. A pickup truck moved slowly down the street, and in front of Felipe's house, a tarp flipped out of the bed, and three men raised automatic weapons.

"My wife and I were lucky!" He shouted and pounded the desk. "Two of my men were not!"

Lucy rolled back into her chair. "Oh my God, what is going on?"

"That's not the half of it," Felipe said and continued. "At 8:20 A.M. this morning, my warehouse was torched."

Lucy had a flashback from seeing the fire truck zip by earlier. She wanted to ask, and she didn't have to wait long before Felipe added that it was one of his stash houses. It was an old warehouse that housed cotton bails until loaded on ships. It was a good front. The raw cotton smell overpowered the slight smell the drugs put out.

His voice escalated again, "A fresh load of Colombian gold uncut came in the night before." His face was red, eyes bulging, and he talked through his teeth. "Street value ten million." He sat back in the chair. His hand swiped his face.

Lucy's mind wondered faster than she could keep up. Was her dream true? Someone tried to kill Felipe and put him out of business. The cartel doesn't care what happens to the drugs after they deliver—they just want their money. The one thing that pounded her brain was, luckily, she never knew the location that housed his drugs. If she did, not even Darby could protect her.

"Your friend Big Sally ordered the hit."

Lucy gave it a thought for a second. Her eyes shifted. "This is getting too real," she mumbled.

"What you say, Mama?"

She changed it quickly. "I said it had to come from Bozzano."

"I know," Felipe shot back. "He has no reason to make such a bold move."

The fire in his eyes raged, then he wrenched his hand. Lucy did her best to talk Felipe down. War was not good for the two drug dealers, and it was not good for the city.

"Felipe, we don't need bodies in the street." Lucy tried to get him to look at her, but his mind was seized with anger.

His jaw clenched. "I'll put one in the back of Big Sally's head, and the last thing Bozzano sees will be me as he dies a slow death."

Lucy watched his grim expression turn horrifying. His flared nose, red face, and eyes were blood-red, which would scare the Devil himself. Then he added to his kill list.

"And for Juan Vargas, he'd die a special death."

There was no talking Felipe down when he was in a rage, and his mind was made up. He stormed out of Lucy's private entrance to an awaiting elevator and disappeared without further disruption.

Lucy spun around in her desk chair. "What have I done?"

CHAPTER 13

A FEW HOURS INTO the prime business hours at the Black Cat Strip Bar, an SUV pulled into the back parking lot. Slowly it pulled through the newly laid asphalt.

"The lot came out good," Felipe said as he exited the car and followed one of his crew with another man behind.

"Your cousin did a nice job," the man leading said.

"Did he treat me right?"

"I'd say so," he said, turning to Felipe. "No cash out of pocket, but he might come to you for a favor one day."

"It works for me," Felipe said, walking in the back entrance of the kitchen.

The cooks and assistants glanced quickly and then turned and tended to food preparation. They never made eye contact with Felipe—that's how they were trained. He had a little swag to his walk and came out of the kitchen into the main bar. A booth remained open even when Felipe was in prison. It was considered a VIP booth used for favors granted or to hustle someone into working for Felipe. This evening Mark and Clark sat waiting, and Felipe slipped into the seat across from the two brothers.

As soon as Felipe sat, the waitress wearing the minimum

the law allowed when not dancing on the stage, placed a bucket of champagne in the center of the table. She popped the cork professionally, not allowing any spillage, and poured three glasses.

In a casino, the dealer watches the player, a pit person watches the dealer, and the eye in the sky watches over everyone. A nightclub is about the same. The girl giving the lap dance watches the patron's hands, and the bouncer protects all the dancers. The eye in the sky looked over the entire club and communicated to the bouncer by radio if there was a problem he missed.

Felipe got the bouncer's attention with his hand in the air. The man knew of his boss's request with a gesture to the music speakers. A nod from security acknowledged Felipe, and soon after, the music was cranked louder.

"Gentlemen," Felipe said, placing his hands on top of theirs. "Thank you for squeezing the information from Clay Morrow. And I might add…without an issue." His head cocked to one side. "Well, at least the incident didn't hit the newspapers."

Clark smiled, "we can be pretty persuasive."

With a slight fist bounce to the table, Felipe smiled. "*Gracias.*" He raised his champagne glass. "To Mark and Clark." Then the brothers joined in, and the three downed the champagne with one gulp.

The waitress poured another round and then stepped away. She stood nearby until Felipe motioned for her to move further away.

Felipe smoothed the leather tabletop with his hands. It was his way of gathering his thoughts before telling a story.

NIGHT TERRORS

He hired Mark and Clark twice, and both were out-of-town jobs. That way, Felipe was far from the crime scene, and it was a good defense for his attorneys. Still, most law enforcement had a pulse on his activity and the knowledge of his reach to any city.

His story took the brothers down the history of Felipe Cruz. As a child from Cuba, he came to the States with his parents and grandfather at five years old.

He knew his grandfather as a doctor living in Cuba. He was gathered up during the night, put on a boat, and slowly crossed the water to the United States. It's the way the story was told to him. He didn't remember all the earlier details. All the riches his family had in Cuba were gone. The only way out of Cuba alive was to leave everything behind.

His father chose the life of crime to put food on the table. Felipe followed in his footsteps and was in and out of detention centers. Then he was charged as an adult and served three years in prison.

He went into detail about how he came from poverty to being a millionaire. He laughed, admitting it didn't matter how he got to be a millionaire or how many people were killed on his way up the ladder. His point was simple: he came from nothing, and no government or person would ever take his fortune and means away.

"No one!" he shouted, pounding his fist on the table. The music covered the sound of his rage. But it caught the attention of the two brothers.

"How much do you think it is worth to protect my income of one hundred million a year?"

Mark looked Clark's way with a blank stare. "I'm not sure what you mean, Felipe."

"How much is it worth for me to protect my investment?" Felipe gave a stern, angry look. "How much? A million, maybe two million dollars?" Felipe bent in closer as if anyone could hear him over the music. "I want you to take out my competition."

"You're putting a bounty of a million dollars on someone?" Mark asked.

Clark quickly added, "Must be a special person."

"Two people. That's why I'm offering so much."

Mark sat back in the booth. His eyes wandered to Clark—then to Felipe. "Who are you talking about?"

Felipe looked around as if someone could hear him. "Tony Bozzano and Big Sally Ricci." His stare sent chills even through men who killed for a living.

Clark spoke when Mark raised his hand in front and cut him off. "No, we're signing our death sentence, which will create a war. No telling how much money will be spent to find the person who took them out." He looked at the ceiling, and the colored lights flashed to the beat of the music. Then he bent over the table into Felipe's face and spoke. "No!"

Felipe went into a sales pitch of why such an amount was offered. Enough for the two to disappear to some island and never return to the States and live comfortably under palm trees and sunny skies for the rest of their life.

Then he threw in a bonus offer. "Other than Sally, Tony has no one else in line to run the operation."

"There is no one local that can step in Tony's place.

Maybe New York will send someone down and maybe not," Clark said.

"What's your beef with Tony?" Mark asked. "Gambling, prostitution, strong-arming, and skimming cash from his legit businesses. He's not interfering with you."

"Bozzano is getting greedy. Looking to partner up with Juan Vargas and take over the drug business."

Mark knocked back a glass of champagne and then leaned into Felipe's face. "We take out Bozzano and Big Sally, so what? Vargas is looking for who took out his partner."

Even with the dim lighting and colors flashing, Felipe's nasty grin showed clearly. It was silence for the moment among them all.

"That's why I'm offering a bonus of another million dollars," Felipe said, then sucked up the rest of his champagne. "Take all three of them out."

Mark and Clark were frozen in time, and neither moved nor spoke. It took a lot to stun these two killers, but Felipe pulled it off.

A bodyguard stepped forward and whispered in Felipe's ear. His eyes shifted, and he quickly stood.

"Gentlemen, think it over. I must go," Felipe said.

Leaning across the table face to face with the brothers, he stared them in the eyes. "Take as long as you want," then he gave off his nasty grin again. "But get back to me by tomorrow evening. You really don't have a choice. I selected you two because you're the best. It's either you take the job, or you're dead."

That night Mark and Clark scouted out some places they could take out Bozzano and planned how Big Sally would respond when he heard the boss was dead. They calculated his moves and how they would take Sally out.

They were back at it early the following morning while sitting in the car, eyeballing the corner location of what looked like an old warehouse. It served its purpose inside a fancy restaurant and casino. It was Bozzano's biggest moneymaker.

"You think we can take him out at his own restaurant?" Clark asked.

"It's where he least expects," Mark replied, his eyes glued on a guy coming from the front door and staring at their vehicle. He reached for his gun from a shoulder holster and placed it on the seat.

"The issue is, we'll never get past the front door with guns strapped to our sides." Mark continued to watch the man until he disappeared, turning the corner. "Go check this guy out. Be sure he didn't make us."

Clark cocked his gun, put a bullet in the chamber, and reached for an extra clip in the console. He opened the door, and his eyes remained glued to the street corner. Crossing the street, he rested his hand on the gun hanging from a holster inside his coat when the man reappeared.

Pushing a hand truck, the man passed Clark. "Good morning."

With a nod of his head, Clark shot back, "Morning." Back at the car, he slipped into the passenger seat. "It's a linen service delivering to Bozzano's club."

They drove to the French Quarter and checked out Bozzano's office location. They knew it was behind the fruit stand but had never been inside to see the layout.

"There are only two options," Mark said. "Take him down coming out of the office or at the warehouse."

Clark rubbed his face with his hand. "Either way, there will be a lot of muscle with him."

"May have to take down more than three targets," Mark said, chewing on his lip. "Could be tricky."

They staked out the office and saw Big Sally come in and open the fruit stand. Shortly after, a blacked-out SUV pulled to the curb. Two men got out with their hands inside their coats. A nod of one's head and the driver opened the door to the back seat. Bozzano stepped out and walked between the two bodyguards.

"From the rooftop across the street, we could kill the boss man and the bodyguards and even take out the driver." Clark made the first push to accept the deal.

"When the boss drops, the place will go on lockdown," Mark said. "Big Sally and Vargas will hide until New York can send help. We must hit them simultaneously and be at the airport within ten minutes."

They did surveillance on the restaurant and casino warehouse for more observation of the daily routine of the Bozzano crew. He parked down the street so he could see the front and rear entrance of the building.

The first option on the table they agreed on was Big Sally, and Bozzano had to be inside. It was easy enough with only two entrances, and then they would go in through the kitchen, guns blazing.

They discussed each would wear overcoats to conceal AK-47's strapped over their shoulders. That would be supplemented by a Glock, tactical belt with extra clips, a smoke bomb, and two hand grenades. Their game plan was that if they went down, everyone went with them.

Mark looked at his watch for the second time.

"I know we have to make a decision," Clark said.

Neither expressed concern with Felipe's threat if they didn't accept the job. He would have to come at them with an army and firepower to take these two down.

They put other options on the table, including drawing Juan to the French Market fruit stand and taking them down from a rooftop.

Mark looked once again at his watch. "Let's go squeeze Felipe. My thoughts are—he'll pay a lot more."

CHAPTER 14

ONE PHONE CALL TO Felipe, and a meeting was set at the strip club between Mark and Clark. The reason for the meeting, Mark explained, was to learn a little more about Tony Bozzano's habits. He suggested anyone should come who could add some insight on the mob boss's daily activities like dinner, entertainment, family, friends, and frequent locations he visited.

The brothers arrived at the club a little after 10 P.M. From the parking lot, they heard the muffled music coming from inside. When opening the front entrance door, the sounds of music were deafening. They made eye contact with the guard at the door, and he frisked them and found an empty shoulder holster strapped to both the brothers.

"We know the drill," Mark said. "Do you really think we'd try to walk in with a piece?"

A nod to another guard, and they walked to Felipe's table.

A waitress arrived topless in the club uniform. She placed an iced-down bucket of champagne and glasses at the center of the table. Felipe appeared shortly after but not without bodyguards.

Mark opened the conversation the best he could over the music, and Felipe cut him off by raising his hand.

"Not yet. I have someone else coming."

The brothers looked at each other, their eyes twitched, and they slipped their hands inside their coats out of habit only to find an empty holster. It was a common practice when something didn't look or feel right to make sure they were not surprised.

Casually, Mark ran his hand down to his boot. It was custom-made and felt, if touched, just like thick leather. Inside a pocket housed a stub-nose .38. For Clark, it was a knife.

"What are we waiting for, Felipe?"

He stared at Mark. "You asked to have someone join us that could give information on Tony Bozzano. Well, here she comes."

Darby did her best to talk Lucy out of going to the meeting. It was too dark inside, the loud music too distracting, and the number of thugs Felipe traveled with made her uncomfortable. She walked in front of Lucy through the maze of people.

Taking a seat, Lucy acknowledged the gentlemen with a pleasant smile.

"Mark and Clark, meet Lucinda Jones," Felipe said.

"Nice to put a face to your names," Lucy replied. She wasn't a fan of the murdering brothers but was happy to finally get a look at them.

Mark's expression went blank with a roll of his eyes. "She's going to help with Bozzano?"

Lucy returned an equally nasty look. "Obviously,

you don't know my power in this town. Felipe called the meeting. Out of respect, I showed, and that doesn't mean I agree to help."

Lucy didn't take lightly anyone disrespecting her and shot him down quickly.

The topless waitress appeared and poured glasses of champagne.

Lucy refused champagne. She then eyeballed the half-naked woman from head to waist. "Aren't you chilly?" When the topless waitress didn't catch Lucy's sarcasm, she didn't comment further.

"I think we all need clear heads where this conversation is going, so you three go light on the bubbly."

The three men drank, and without saying Felipe had ordered a hit on his competition, Lucy knew where the conversation was going.

"Why am I here?" Lucy said, getting in Felipe's face. "Why are you getting me tangled up with these two? Just meeting with all of you could have consequences. It could take our empire down. Do you understand?"

Lucy listened while Felipe chatted…or, as Lucy referred to his long, drawn-out stories, "going around the block." He finally asked if she could help with Bozzano's habits. Maybe a fishing camp, hunting, a visit to Club Twilight, anything that might pinpoint him in a location?

"Well, he certainly was never at Club Twilight," Lucy said. "He had the pick of the litter at his own stable. Not sure why he ever let Vivian operate. She was in direct competition with him, and yet he never said a word when I took her business over."

It took a while, and Felipe finally asked. "Lucy, if you were to plan to take down Bozzano, Big Sally, and Juan," he said and paused. "What's your best move?" He saw Lucy physically draw back at the question. Her face was flush, and she messed with her hair over her shoulders. Felipe knew her behaviors when nervous.

"Little Mama, all your cash is coming to a dead stop." Felipe did that thing with his lips that Lucy hated. "You may have all the money you need right now. But sooner are later, it's all going to hit the fan, and you'll need tons of cash to keep your sweet ass out of prison."

"Is that a threat?"

"No, Mama," Felipe gave that look again. "I want to keep you in the lifestyle you're accustomed to, and I don't want your money train to stop. Just help me out?"

"You're far from concerned about me," Lucy shot back, never afraid to speak her mind even to a big murdering drug lord like Felipe. "You need millions coming in to keep paying your crew, judges, expensive lawyers, and most of all..." She stopped and questioned herself if she should go on. She hesitated but continued. "It's not about the money. It's Juan taking over your territory. It's pride. You'll look like a failure to all your gang bangers. One by one, they will turn on you. Felipe, you need to control the drug business for more than the money. Control brings respect, which is more important to you than anything."

Before Lucy could say another word, Felipe reached across the table and snatched her forearm, pulling her off the seat. "Nobody talks to me like that."

Darby caught Felipe's move on Lucy and stepped to the back of him away from the bodyguard's view. "Gently let her arm go, or the blade I have to your back will puncture your lung," She whispered in his ear. Darby reacted, pushing the blade through his jacket, pricking his skin with the point. He quickly released Lucy's arm.

She patted Felipe on the shoulder and stepped away. Darby was so smooth that the brothers and bodyguards were unaware that their boss had come close to death.

"*Te tallarè como un cerdo*—" Felipe shouted out to Darby as she stepped away.

Her eyes locked on Felipe. "Take your best shot." She knew little Spanish but that she had heard before. They were his crew's favorite words. *I'll carve you like a pig.*

Lucy stood. "I'll be in touch." Then she walked behind Darby's back through the maze of dancers. She was doing that thing with her eyes as they shifted from side to side. It was her way of processing things. Then she tapped Darby's shoulder and whispered the best she could over the music. They made an about-face, and Darby had difficulty keeping up with Lucy back to the table.

"I'll lay a plan out for you. But I promise if you screw this up, I will put a bullet into all your heads," Lucy said, sliding into the booth next to Felipe.

"Bozzano has a granddaughter, Annamaria, who goes to Saint Anthony's School on Canal Street."

"I don't kill kids," Mark spit out quickly.

"On the contrary," Lucy said. "If a hair on her head is so much as out of place, both of you are dead." Her eyes followed their reaction like daggers. "The granddaughter is an avenue to Bozzano, and she walks away untouched and doesn't see you take her grandfather out."

Felipe nodded his head up and down. "Might work. We kidnap the kid and demand Bozzano and Juan to be at the drop. Ask for little money. Fifty grand, he'll have that in his safe."

"He's not coming without Big Sally," Lucy said. "So, you have your shot at all three."

"It's up to you two," Felipe said, nodding at the brothers.

"That's my input, and remember, the kid walks away—untouched." She stared them down, then walked away, her hand stretched out to Darby's back. They cut through the crowded floor as if they were dancing and made it out front.

"What the hell, Lucy?" Darby said at the car. "You put that child in harm's way."

"I'm keeping my enemies close," she said and smiled. "They wanted my input but will never react to my suggestions."

Darby's head cocked to one side. "So why come to the meeting?"

"We put a face to the brothers." She paused. "Sooner or later, Felipe will give the order for them to take me out. You've been introduced to who you'll have to kill before they get to me."

CHAPTER 15

Lucy could think of only one other occasion when she thought of going totally legit. With various revenue streams and an offer to sell the salon and the building only if Club Twilight came with the deal, she told herself she was working towards that goal but wasn't ready to pull the trigger.

The music beat from the nightclub lasted in Lucy's ears until they pulled into the gates of her Lakefront home. The gates automatically closed behind the vehicle, and the garage doors opened. The SUV parked, and Darby pressed the button to close the garage doors before Lucy exited the car.

It was a process Darby insisted on to protect Lucy. She had many friends but just as many enemies. Telling her *if you will not use the security setup, why was it installed?* That was Darby's answer when Lucy tried to use her authority.

Lucy's guts turned; she knew it would be a long night. Her stomach was shaky ever since she put Bozzano's granddaughter in harm's way. It popped into her head, and she spewed out her thoughts like her father did often without thinking. He would have suggested something on that order and was famous for throwing minors into the mix to make the con work.

Once, he robbed a bank and took a child. Outside, his partner sat in a car with the motor running. Had the police caught up with him, the child would have been thrown from the vehicle. His logic behind the move was the police would stop to take care of the child. He never worried the kid would get broken bones or be run over by the police car. It was whatever it took for him to get away.

One day after school, he picked Lucy up. That should have been a tip-off—he never picked her up unless he had a con working. He had worked with her on jumping out of a car at an old, abandoned farm for weeks. Jump and roll, he taught her. The day he picked her up from school, he robbed a supermarket and had her with a school bag walking out front back and forth until he came out waving his gun and scooped her up in his arms. People screamed and shouted. *He took the little girl.* If the police came after him, Lucy's cue was to jump from the moving car. Luckily it wasn't necessary, and she was dropped off.

Making her way back to the supermarket, she'd describe the robber, which was always different from the description the witnesses in the grocery described. Lucy was taught what to say. *Were you close to the man enough to know he had blue eyes and sandy brown hair, a little gray on the sides? Because I know who grabbed me and stuffed me into the car.*

She knew how to misdirect the police and cry on the spot too.

Then she'd tell the police about another man—the driver. But there was no other man. Her father drove, and it was all a story to keep the police looking at many suspects.

Lucy knew her brain housed all the nasty details her father taught her and had to keep them buried and not react when they came forward.

"Darby," Lucy shouted on her way down the stairs to change into something comfortable. She found Darby in the kitchen making her usual late-night snack. "Need a cocktail."

"A nightcap outside?" Wild-eyed Darby suggested. She was always ready for a cocktail around the fire pit on the patio.

"It works for me," Lucy said and headed outside.

While working for Lucy for only a few years, Darby knew her process. Something was bugging her, and her job was to make Lucy come clean.

"I never knew your father," Darby said. "But I wish he wasn't dead."

Lucy shot her a side glance. "Why?"

"Because I'd like to take him out myself. Real slow, too. There is a special place in hell for your father."

Lucy laughed, but Darby was dead serious.

They discussed the chances of Mark and Clark using the child to get Bozzano and Juan in the same place over a cocktail. Which turned into three into the early morning. Their heads whirled from the cocktails and partly from hashing over the same subject for hours.

The following day Lucy came downstairs to the smell of coffee and hot biscuits. Living in the big house could not have happened without Darby. She was always up first, had coffee brewed, and prepared an old family recipe for breakfast most mornings. Darby prepared her favorite sweet potato biscuits.

They were halfway into the first cup of coffee when Lucy got a text. *Guns on the move tonight,* it read.

Lucy sat back in the lounge chair and looked up at the morning sun coming over the trees. "Why does this guy make the guns my problem?"

"Hopefully, the guns ship out of state," Darby said, heading to the stove to check the biscuits. "Not that it's good for that much firepower to land in any city."

Another text came through. *I need to talk to you.*

"What the hell?" Lucy said. "This guy is pushing his luck with me." Then she waved her cup to Darby.

"Ms. Councilwoman, the pot is on the counter," Darby pointed.

"What kind of restaurant is this?" She took the clue and poured her own coffee. "Oh yes!" She let out a squeal when the sweet potato biscuits passed under her nose. Still hot when cutting, Lucy smeared honey and butter inside.

"How are the biscuits?" Darby asked.

"An extra four hours at the gym," she replied. "That's how good."

Darby rarely got involved or ask questions regarding Lucy's business unless she brought the subject up. Concerned where the guns might land, she butted in and dug.

"Couldn't you hint to someone on the police force about the guns?" Darby said it and waited.

Lucy finished the biscuit, touched up her fingers

from the sticky honey, then gave a slight smile. "Are you suggesting I drop a hint to Stella?"

"Well, she is a cop." Darby tried to keep a straight face—it didn't work.

"Yeah, she's a cop who worked in drug enforcement and was involved in gang-related crimes."

"There you go," Darby grinned. "Direct her to Mr. John, and he's off your back."

She reached for another biscuit. "Damn you! I am going to be in the gym for a week."

Other than running into Stella at City Hall, she had not spoken to her since the blow-up over eight months ago. She also threw out there the possibility that Stella probably had a new girlfriend.

Darby assured her she wasn't seeing anyone. Then she broke the news she had run into Stella the last week at the coffee shop.

The biscuit hit the plate, slipping out of Lucy's hand. At first, she was upset that Darby had not told her about running into Stella. Then it whirled around in her head, and all she could muster up was, "Really? She's not seeing anyone?"

Lucy put on her stern face and bitched Darby out for holding back information, especially about an ex-lover. Then she slowed down, asking: How did she look?

"She cut her hair," Darby threw out as a distraction, but it didn't work.

"I know, Lucy said. "I saw her at City Hall the other day. It floored me—she loved her long hair."

"She said one morning she just got tired of ponytails

and dealing with the long hair," Darby said, rolling her eyes. "She looks great, not that she ever looked bad." Darby stepped in like a sister and suggested: "Is it wrong to ask Stella for help as a concerned citizen?"

Lucy leaned on the back two legs of the dining room chair, something she got on other people for doing.

There wasn't much more spoken on the subject, and Darby, from experience, knew to leave it alone. Lucy would come around when she was ready.

Darby cleaned the kitchen while Lucy checked her phone messages and called John back. She never liked texting for long conversations, especially with unsavory people.

John answered and thanked her for calling. They set a meeting at Café Beignet on Royal Street. It was within walking distance to John's business and around the corner from where the guns were stored. Not that it made a difference, Lucy had no intentions of taking this on herself. She wanted to keep a merchant happy and maybe get him some help with her connections.

Darby freshened up. There was not much to do with her hair—it was shorter than most men sported. She flipped on a camouflage cap which matched her pants. A handgun went in a holster on her belt, and a nine-inch switchblade went in her pocket. It was all legal to carry unless she escorted Lucy to her office. Weapons were not allowed in City Hall, and everyone went through screening.

Darby pulled the SUV around to the circular drive and waited. Directed to get the car to the front entrance did not necessarily mean Lucy would be waiting when Darby arrived. She'd take a phone call on her way out, half-dressed with one arm in her coat, the other holding the phone.

When the shiny black SUV pulled curbside at the café, tourists stopped and watched. The narrow Royal Street housed the Eighth District Police Station in the block and mainly had police cars parked.

The big SUV stood out, and people watched as if a celebrity had arrived. Darby held Lucy's hand as she slipped from the seat to the ground. People mumbled and threw out random Hollywood names among themselves with some being far-fetched. Darby always got a chuckle out of the craziness. When Lucy opened her coordinating umbrella blocking the sun, you could hear the shrilling sounds among the viewers.

"Folks? It's just Lucy from Tupelo," Darby said, offering a broad smile.

Lucy became accustomed to being made over, and she grew to like it. After all, what women don't like attention? Lucy was the Queen of Con and used her smile and beautiful figure to lure enemies closer and gain their confidence. Some things she couldn't shake from her early con days with her father. She was once the cute little girl that distracted people so Edgar could shoplift, and now all grown up, she took advantage of men to the point they forgot their own names.

"Let's go, Darby," Lucy said. "Let's see what John's all about."

CHAPTER 16

INSIDE THE COFFEE SHOP, Lucy found John sitting in the garden area. It was a secluded area where she had specifically directed him when setting up the meeting.

"Ms. Lucy," John said, standing and then pulling a chair out for her.

Coffee was delivered, and Lucy passed on the beignets. She was wearing black pants—a no-no to the puffballs of powdered sugar. When biting into the dough—most of the powdered sugar stuck to your lips and fell on your clothes. Still, people loved their beignets.

Lucy sipped her coffee while John talked in-between eating. He showed her a picture on his phone of Beth Wiggins standing in front of guns stacked on racks. Beth claimed she heard her father on the phone telling someone the guns were ready for pickup. A disagreement broke out, and she listened to her father raging. *Enough is enough.*

"Why have you made this your problem?" Lucy asked, staring into his eyes. "And why pull me into your drama?"

He didn't blink. "Something terrible is going to happen. I feel it, and I don't want to be a part."

Lucy leaned back and sipped the last of her coffee.

She studied John. He was a good actor or an absolute liar. Something didn't add up, but she couldn't put her finger on it.

"I believe the guns will move tomorrow morning," John said.

"Dammit, how can you be so sure? Tomorrow morning?"

John became angry and stood throwing money on the table for the coffee and beignets. "I am a concerned citizen, and I thought you could help without me going to the police." He pushed a chair out of the way. The iron legs made a dreadful sound on the slate flooring of the garden area. "Thank you for nothing."

Lucy sat, ordered more coffee, and called Darby to join her. Her mind checked out by the time she arrived.

"Hello," she said. "Lucy?"

"Sorry," Lucy said. "I zoned out. This John guy? Something doesn't add up."

Rehashing the conversation only confused things more when Darby added her two cents. A conspiracy theorist, she could turn around and twist things to make anyone believe any theory, and it drove Lucy crazy.

"Sorry I added you to the fold, Darby. That only confuses me more."

A quick hash over the little they both knew of John proved he had only arrived as a merchant in the French Quarter less than a year ago.

"Call a PI we know and trust." Lucy said. "See what he can find on this guy."

Darby smiled, "I have a better idea. Ask the detective that just walked in."

Lucy turned to the garden entrance, and there she was in her navy blue suit with the white shirt buttoned to the top. Looking as sharp as ever, so professional, and yet knowing she had a gun strapped to her side made it sexy.

"Hello Stella," Lucy said, greeting her with a broad smile. Watching her former lover stroll towards her, Lucy turned to Darby. "I am going to kill you."

"I didn't call her," Darby defended. "What the hell! You're the one that took a meeting next to the police station."

She pulled the chair out. "Take my seat, Stella. I was just leaving."

"Hello Lucy," Stella said and gave her a kiss on the cheek.

Lucy pointed. "Please have a seat."

Stella sat but said she couldn't stay. She was meeting someone.

Lucy mulled over John's conversation and was tempted to add Stella to Darby's theory. Fighting with herself, she always asked Stella for favors when calling her out of the blue. But this time, they just bumped into each other.

Squirming in the seat like a teenager, she smiled. "You look great, and I love your short hair."

Stella flipped the ends of her hair. "Yeah, I like it. Easier to keep up with, especially when I get a call in the middle of the night."

Lucy fought with herself not to ask for another favor, but she lost. "Stella, if I give you a name, could you check and see if he is on anybody's radar?"

"You know I can't do that," she said, watching Lucy's smile fade.

A long pause came, then Stella whipped out a notepad. "Of course, I can, for you," she said, placing the pad and pen on the table.

Lucy quickly wrote John Davis's name down and passed the pad back and stopped. Then she wrote Cole Wiggins's name.

Lucy said, handing the pad to Stella, "Thank you so much. I'm thinking of doing business with these two and can't find any background on them."

"I have to go," Stella said. "That's my friend." She motioned to a woman at the entrance dressed in a similar suit. "I'll let you know if I get anything on these two. You look great, honey," Stella said. Her eyes sparkled, then gave a wink. "We need to do lunch—and catch up."

Lucy was surprised and stood stunned. Her response was way after Stella stepped away. "Yes, I'd like that."

She watched Stella greet the woman. There was no kiss, no pulling the chair out like she would have done for her when they were dating.

"It must be a friend, not a lover," she whispered. Then Lucinda surfaced. *What's the issue? You don't want Stella, but no one else can have her, either? Maybe you haven't gotten over her yet?*

"Shut the hell up, Lucinda, and get out of my head," she said. From the reaction of a table of four nearby, she spoke way too loudly. Lucy gave her broadest smile and flashed her eyelashes as she passed the table of ladies. "You girls, have a nice day."

Whispering came from the table as she strolled past, using the umbrella as a walking cane.

"Wasn't that the lady they call Voodoo Lucy?" One lady asked.

Lucy added a little more swag to her walk when she heard it. Meeting Darby curbside, she stepped into the open door of the SUV, but it was not before waving to the ladies in the garden area who still had their eyes locked on her.

Lucy read one lady's lips and was sure she said, "Yep, that's Voodoo Lucy."

Darby caught Lucy with a surprised look on her face. "What are you grinning about?"

"I'm just amazed," Lucy said. "Who would have thought a kid from Tupelo could reach celebrity status. At least in their minds?" She laughed. "They're easily amused."

CHAPTER 17

Simultaneously assassinating two crime bosses took strategic planning. If the job were botched, the culprit would be the one in a body bag. After a considerable discussion and backing out of the deal twice, the brothers agreed to perform the services for a one-million-dollar advance. The balance transfers would go to a third-world bank, which Clark had used for years when his contracted jobs were completed. A few thousand dollars also went to the manager who would make the paper trail disappear.

Two of Felipe's trusted crew walked into the bus station early morning. One man carried a canvas bag, and the other kept a watchful eye with his hand locked on the gun's trigger tucked inside his belt. The gunmen watched his partner place the canvas bag into a locker. The men found the brothers at a coffee counter. They walked up as old friends, and in conversation, one man slipped the locker key into a paper napkin, placing it in front of Clark. The transaction took little time. Clark confirmed the money in the locker, leaving it there until they were ready to get out of town.

The first order of business was to scout Bozzano's

underground Casino and Dinner Club. The brothers sat looking the neighborhood over like they were planning for any job. Escape routes were as crucial as mass slaughters.

After gunfire broke out in the club, leaving the two high-power men dead, everyone would rush the exits, and the brothers wanted to be within the mix. They agreed to exit the front entrance with the crowd of confused people running for safety. Once the guns were tucked under their coats, they would blend with the rest rushing out.

They considered the third person as a getaway driver. The car would be ready, the engine running and prepared to race to the interstate.

The exit strategy was to hit the interstate using only right-hand turns. That would allow the getaway vehicle to take to the walkway if traffic backed up. They monitored the street within one hour of the planned murders to understand the traffic flow.

The assassination was planned for peak time when the club had the loudest music blasting and most people dancing. As professionals, they wanted people running and screaming when bullets fired. The chaos would keep Bozzano's people at bay for fifteen to twenty seconds until the room cleared. By that time, the brothers would be in the car and would have made the first turn toward the highway.

The getaway was clear except for a driver, which Clark had someone in mind. The next step was to figure out how to get inside the club with guns and perform the actual mass murder of Bozzano, Big Sally, and Juan Vargas.

It was mid-morning when Clark saw the linen truck a block away. The same driver they saw days earlier parked in front of a café on Magazine Street. The driver opened the doors to the truck's rear, pulling two towel rolls used for the pulldown machines to dry your hands in bathrooms. He walked into the cafe with a roll under each arm. Minutes later, he returned and drove the truck to Bozzano's building, parking on the side street just like he did every day. Soon after, he came around the corner with a hand truck and linens stacked in plastic boxes.

When Clark watched the linen truck stop at the Café, then move to Bozzano's building, an idea hit him.

"Perfect!" Clark said.

"What?" Mark replied.

"Get my briefcase out of the trunk," Clark said, his eyes locked on the back entrance of the kitchen the linen driver when through.

Mark flopped the briefcase onto the seat. Clark ran the numbers to the combination locks, and the release popped open. He moved two weapons to the side, pulled a leather folder, examined the inside, and smiled.

"What do you have in mind?" Mark asked.

"I think I found the answer."

Clark strolled to the linen truck and waited on the driver's side. Shortly later, the man returned, opened the rear doors, and placed the cart inside, then closed the doors.

"Can I help you?" the driver said, stopping in his tracks, seeing the unexpected man leaning against his truck.

Clark smiled. "Don't be alarmed." Then he flipped the leather folder open. "I am agent Thompson. FBI."

The badge all but put the driver in cardiac arrest. "What is this about?"

"What is your name?"

"Daniel." The driver answered.

"I am on a stakeout and could use your help."

Daniel stood at attention, adjusting his red logo vest the linen company issued as part of a uniform. "My help?"

Clark confirmed two stops on Daniel's route, the café and the warehouse. Making sure it was a daily stop was essential to the plan. Daniel confirmed.

"If I call on you for assistance, can I count on you?" Clark gave a stern look. "Trust you not to tell anyone. Not your wife, a friend—no one!"

"Yes, sir," Daniel said excitedly to be involved.

"Okay, Daniel. If I need you, it will be within a day or two. I am counting on you, and your government depends on you." Clark reached in his pocket and peeled off five one-hundred-dollar bills. "I'm authorized to pay you for your services," and placed the money in his hands. "There will be another five hundred if we call on you."

Daniel was speechless and finally muttered, "Yes, sir." He slipped the money into his pocket.

Clark tapped him on the shoulder as he walked away. "There will be consequences if you tell anyone."

"No, sir! Not a word," Daniel shouted to his back as Clark walked across the street.

As they drove off, Clark turned to Mark, "I found the perfect idiot. This is going to work out fine."

CHAPTER 18

LUCY KEPT A BURNER cell phone, and only two people had the number: Felipe, who seldom called, preferring to talk face to face, and Mayor Sam Algarotti. The phone had thirty minutes of private, non-traceable conversations. That was more time than Lucy wanted to speak to either of them, and when they were finished talking, the cell phone was destroyed.

Lucy sat at a table garden side at the Court of Two Sisters restaurant on Royal Street for a meeting Stella set up. She wasn't sure if it was a makeup brunch to see her or to report on the information Lucy's requested on John Davis.

A muffled ring tone came from her purse. She knew it was the one she programmed for Felipe. Stella was due any second, and she was hesitant to answer. Knowing Felipe, he'd keep calling until she answered. Lucy took the call.

"Not a good time, Felipe," Lucy said without even a hello.

"Don't care," Felipe shot back. "Bozzano will want to show off his underground casino/night club to Juan. Big shot Tony does it with all his new business partners, and I need to know when."

"How the hell am I supposed to get this information," Lucy spewed out. She got a glimpse of Stella at the front podium. "I'll get back to you, Felipe."

"Mama! I'm not one of your employees at the salon. You get back to me pronto with the time and date, and don't ever disrespect me again." The call went dead.

Lucy put the best smile on to greet Stella, but her stomach was making flips. Since Felipe got out of jail, he had been out of control. There was only one person she knew could get that info but digging into it could send three men to their deaths.

"Stella, so nice to see you," Lucy said, standing to accept a kiss from her friend. She slipped the cell phone back into her purse and focused on Stella.

Lucy made small talk doing her best to get a feel for the meeting, not sure if maybe Stella had second thoughts on their on-again, off-again romance. Deep down, Lucy knew she needed Stella in her life, not as much for romance as it was to have a cop in the know at your side.

"You look nice," Stella said.

"What? This old thing?" Lucy shot back rubbing the collar of her jacket.

Stella gave a wrinkled nose look. "That outfit would take a few weeks' salaries to hang in my closet."

"What's on your mind, Stella?" Lucy gave a side glance. "You have that look."

"I don't have a look," Stella insisted. Then she caved. "Lucy, I need to walk you across the street."

"What the hell does that mean?"

Crossing her legs, she leaned into Lucy. "I checked

into that John Davis and his daughter," she said, slightly smiling.

"Yeah?" Lucy asked, her eyes roaming the room nervously.

"It opened a hornet's nest," Stella said. This time she had a cold stone stare. "I was called to the mat by the head of the ATF and DEA who wanted to know how I came across John Davis.

Lucy sat silent. Everything ran through her mind. *Why did she even bring the name up to Stella? Why did she feel a need to get involved with Davis? Then second-guessing, she should have blown the guy off and not called him back.*

"What do you want with me?"

"For now, take a walk and meet with the ATF and DEA."

"You told them Davis's name came from me. What the hell, Stella!" She shouted loud enough to turn heads in the restaurant. "Are you going to cuff me?"

"Lucy, they just want to talk. You're not under arrest," Stella said. "Besides, you like being handcuffed."

Lucy gave a false front and smiled. When nervous, she'd try to crack a joke for diversion. "It's been a long time since you cuffed me," she said, rolling her eyes.

The restaurant was a block and a half down Royal Street from the police station. It was a beautiful morning and reminded Lucy of the times they walked hand and hand window shopping. This time it was all business.

Stella had her tight dark blue cop pants on with a light blue button-down shirt and walked with authority. Much like she was escorting a criminal to jail.

It wasn't until Lucy walked into the police station that she felt pressure. Worried she'd say something wrong, all that ran through her mind was that she was a money launderer for a drug kingpin, getting ready to squeal on a guy with guns in his garage.

Seeing uniforms running around made Lucy uncomfortable, and her wide-eyed reaction caught Stella's attention.

"Here we are," Stella said, opening a small conference room door.

Inside, two men standing greeted Lucy. Shaking hands, they introduced themselves as Commander Wilson Young with ATF and Bradford Scott with Drug Enforcement.

Commander Young motioned. "Please have a seat, Ms. Jones."

She was offered coffee or water, and Lucy took Mr. Young up on a bottle of water. Not that she was thirsty, but she wanted time to compose herself.

Bradford sat while Wilson fetched the water, and Lucy worked on her breathing. Deep breathing exercises her doctor taught her when her anxiety surfaced. By the time Wilson returned with the water, she felt better, and her mind cleared that she had nothing to hide. So, she kept telling herself just answer the questions as they come, and like an attorney drilling you in a courtroom, don't elaborate. Just answer the question, preferably often with a yes or no answer.

"Detective, we'll handle it from here. Thank you for your assistance," Wilson Young said, opening the door for Stella.

NIGHT TERRORS

"Ms. Jones," Wilson said, taking a seat at the table. "How do you know John Davis?"

"He's a merchant in the French Quarter," she quickly shot back. "I'm the Merchant Associations President."

Dammit Lucy! That's not what he asked," Lucinda's voice penetrated Lucy's mind.

Her head spun when asked if she knew anything about John Davis's stockpile of guns. She rolled back her conversation with Stella. The names and guns were never discussed, so there was no wrong answer.

Lucinda, her dark half, rose to the occasion and filled Lucy's head with random thoughts. *Be careful, Lucy. His questions are a trap.*

Lucy didn't answer too quickly. They studied her, waiting for her to blink, look away, or take a deep gulp—all the things law enforcement taught in behavior when interviewing a suspect. Lucy learned her profiling on the street—she was a pro and knew how to confuse them and take charge.

"I'm sorry. Did you say guns?"

"Yes," Wilson said.

Lucy's experience with cops when her father was questioned: they asked the same question several ways to see if you answered differently.

"No, sir, we never talked about guns."

"You told Detective James you were planning on doing business with John Davis and Cole Wiggins."

Lucy's mind took another whirl. *Whose side are you on, Stella.* It ran through her mind, and she tried to control herself by offering a pleasant demeanor.

Smiling, showing her pearly whites, she answered. "As I said, I am the president of the French Quarter Association. The two men planned to create a partnership for a new venture on Royal Street. I just asked Stella to see if they had any criminal records."

"Do you know an Oscar Sanchez?" Commander Wilson asked harshly.

"No, never heard of the man."

Lucy had been down this avenue before. She stood, offered another smile, and stepped to the door. "Gentlemen, you too are too aggressive for me to sit and listen to. Maybe because I'm a woman, you feel you can run over me with your questions, intimidate me, and trick me somehow. Either way, I'm leaving. Any further questioning will go through my attorney."

"Did you know John Davis's real name is Oscar Sanchez?" Wilson blurted out.

Lucy reached for the door handle, then turned back to the men. "No, never heard of Oscar Sanchez. But, thanks for the info, and I think I'll pass on approving him for a business in the French Quarter. Enough criminals run the streets without having a business owner with an alias. Who knows what type of person he is?"

Lucy turned the door handle about to leave and realized. John Davis had reported Wiggins as an arms dealer.

"So, what is the connection between Davis and Wiggins?" Lucy asked.

Wilson gave a side glance over to Bradford, then looked at Lucy and spoke. "I can't tell you anything further."

"You drag my ass in here, pump me with questions,

and can't answer a simple question?" Lucy came across just the way she felt. "I just wanted to know if they are business partners and suitable as merchants in the French Quarter."

There was silence for the longest time, then Wilson spoke. "They are partners with different ideas of moving forward." He paused as if he was choosing his words carefully. "Let's say one is evil, and the other guy is worse."

Commander Wilson stood and reached for Lucy's hand. "Sorry if I offended you. Something is about to go down, and we need to find the guns. We thought you might know something."

"I run a beauty salon, and I mind my business other than when wives complain about their cheating husbands. I do love juicy gossip." She shrugged her shoulders. "What do I know about gun dealers?" Lucy offered another fake smile. "It's been a pleasure, gentlemen." She left the room, her head about to explode.

Walking to the front entrance, she glimpsed Stella at a desk in conversation with another police officer. Stella smiled as she passed. Lucy didn't acknowledge her. It wasn't the time or the place for her to address the issue, but she made a mental note. Stella was a cop first, and friendship was way down the list. Having a cop in your back pocket for information was one thing, but a snitch was another.

Lucy walked Royal Street at the peak of throngs of tourists and street performers. She was not in the mood for any of them or the noise when her name was called. It was faint over the sound of "When the Saints Come Marching In," one of the many songs street bands played.

A hand-pulled Lucy from her shoulder. "Lucy!" Stella

said, catching up to her. She pulled Lucy around a corner away from the police station by the hand.

"You're being watched."

"For sure, and thanks to you for filling them in on what they didn't know.

"All I did was mention Davis and Wiggins's name—as you asked. I was questioned on who inquired. When I said your name, the conversation got intense."

"Why?"

"I don't know for sure," Stella said, her eyes got runny. "How are you involved with these people?"

"I told you they want to join the merchant's associations," Lucy said, sticking to her story.

"Bradford said Felipe Cruz, Davis, and Wiggins were all on the radar," Stella said and gave a death stare.

"Are you sure?"

"One hundred percent," Stella said, holding firmly to Lucy's arm. "The DEA said it would be a good time to bring you in—they are connecting you to Felipe."

Lucy's heart sunk then she remembered what she had learned from her father. *When you're backed against the wall, lie. The bigger the lie, the better.*

"Yeah, Stella. I'm involved with a scumbag drug lord. You guessed it, I'm his go-to person. He gives the word, and I'll put two to the back of your head. Want drugs? I am his mule too. Want it by the ounce or by the pound? I'm your girl."

"Real funny, Lucy. I'm telling you, as a friend, I don't know why they are looking at you—but they sure jumped at the chance to bring you in for questioning."

"Well, thanks for the heads up." She tried to play nice and gave Stella a wink. "Keep me posted on this witch hunt."

CHAPTER 19

LUCY'S THOUGHTS RAN RAPIDLY on the walk back to the salon. She fought with herself that Stella was telling the truth. If John Davis and Cole Wiggins were on the radar of the DEA and ATF, Stella really wouldn't be involved.

Stella was a homicide detective and not in the know of ongoing investigations with other agencies. It's what she kept telling herself.

Her throwaway phone vibrated at the bottom of her purse. Looking at the phone number on the screen, it was Felipe.

Lucy answered, "Hello."

"Mama, where is my information?" He said, not so pleasantly.

"Felipe, you need to cool your jets. I am working on it," she said. "I was just beat down by the police, and there are some things you need to hear."

"Who are you talking with, Stella, your cop friend?" Felipe shot back. "I thought you had her under control?"

"No cop is totally under control, not even the ones you have on your payroll," Lucy said. She knew how to be tough with Felipe and put him in his place, and she would not be intimidated by him.

"So, what did the cops want?"

"Not locals. The ATF and DEA." She let that settle in for a second. "You know an Oscar Sanchez?"

There was a long pause. "I can't say I do."

"Well, this guy is a gun runner and has a stockpile of weapons in your backyard." Felipe's quietness showed he was evidently concerned, so Lucy hit him again.

"What about John Davis?"

"Come on, Lucy, pick up the phone book. There are thousands of 'Davis' names in this city."

"Well, John Davis and Oscar are the same," she said. "That's what the ATF has been drilling me about for the last hour."

Felipe shot off questions without a pause. "Alcohol, Tobacco, Firearms? How are you involved with ATF?"

"I don't know, Felipe. I stumbled across this, and it's got me worried. Something is going down with guns, and it might just be arms deal or a takedown. Either way I don't need a war on my streets. Enough said, meet me in an hour at location six."

Felipe repeated, "Location six."

"Kill your phone, and I'll do the same," Lucy said. She took the battery out and snapped the flip-top phone, breaking the connection. Half the phone went in the drain where thousands of Mardi Gras beads went to rest, and the other half she lobbed in the back of a passing garbage truck.

CHAPTER 20

THE SUV PARKED ON Royal Street at the salon entrance, and Darby stood at the rear passenger's door.

"Tony Bozzano's fruit stand," Lucy rattled off, getting in the back seat.

"Did you enjoy your walk?" Darby said, starting the engine.

"Don't ask. It's not been a good day."

Darby asked nothing further and drove. She knew Lucy's moods too well.

It took no time to get over to Chartres Street. The 18-wheeler produce trucks were long gone unloading, and the daily retail merchant's pickups were back at their grocery stores. This was when tourists flooded the unique fresh market on foot.

Darby parked in front of Bozzano's vegetable stands, and Lucy stepped to the curb. Gathering her thoughts for the best story to tell, she reached for tomatoes looking each one over carefully, then placing a few in a brown paper bag. She ran through her story a few times while looking at the camera. It would only be a minute before Big Sally approached. His main job was to watch the monitors in the office, and another employee handled retail. Sally watched for suspicious people and those with a connection to Bozzano.

The mirage of a door opened, hidden in the mural, and Big Sally appeared. "Don't squeeze the tomatoes, lady."

Lucy smelled in the bag. "Sweet tomatoes."

"You know Mr. B gets the best." He smiled. "Shopping? I know you don't have an appointment."

"I came personally to ask Mr. B for a sit-down. Maybe at his restaurant?"

"I'll see if he can meet you at Luna's for lunch this week."

"No," Lucy said. "I need a lot of noise for this discussion. Dinner at the warehouse nightclub."

Sally's big bushy eyebrows went up, and he thought for a second. Lucy stared him down. "Sally, this is important. There is some heavy stuff going down in the city, and he needs to know."

"What kind of stuff?" Sally's job was to get much information before approaching his boss for an appointment. He was good at what he did.

"DEA and ATF kind of business. Must be soon," Lucy pushed as hard as she could without Sally realizing she was fishing for Bozzano's whereabouts.

"I know he's meeting tomorrow night with clients," Sally said, giving his boyish smile. It was the smile he did when flirting with her. "I'll see if I can get you in an hour before."

Lucy pulled Sally from the view of the camera. Reaching in her purse, she pulled two one-hundred-dollar bills. "See what you can do." She stuck the money in his hand. "You know I appreciate your help."

Lucy placed the bag on the scale.

Sally reached and gave it back to her. "Enjoy there on the house. Make a nice tomato sandwich."

"You're too kind," Lucy said, playing Sally as she always did when needing something from him.

Darby opened the rear door for Lucy. As she got in, she made eye contact with Sally. "Sally, make it happen. As I said, it's important."

He shot her another smile, "I'll see what I can do.'"

CHAPTER 21

Location six was the old Pontchartrain Beach parking lot on Lakeshore Drive, not far from Lucy's mansion. It was a wide-open space, and Lucy and Felipe would feel comfortable talking. It was one of many sites Lucy set up. They mixed them up a lot, so the police could not set up surveillance in time.

"Pontchartrain Beach," Lucy said from the back seat.

Darby wasted no time getting there and pulled into the parking lot and parked. Soon after, three SUV Suburbans with blacked-out windows drove up. The back doors of all three vehicles opened, and six men stood. They did not look like they were armed, but Darby assured Lucy that weapons were nearby.

One man walked Felipe to Lucy's vehicle and opened the rear door. Then he stepped in and took a seat. A glass-tinted partition came up for privacy between the driver and passengers.

"Well, Mama, we got ourselves a problem?"

Lucy looked at the pictures of guns John forwarded to her. She flipped the images in front of Felipe. She explained the girl in the photo, then talked about how John Davis was an alias, and the ATF believed his real name might be Oscar Sanchez.

"This guy played me," she said. "I will get even with this bastard. He said he discovered the guns through his daughter who is friends with Beth Wiggins. Made it sound like he was a concerned citizen."

Felipe said little. He was the person who listened to every detail and then added his opinion.

"That's why I don't have partners," Felipe said. "With partners, there are always egos, attitudes, or some bullshit that gets in the way. Whatever his name is, Davis or Sanchez, he had other ideas about what he wanted to do with the guns."

"Think it's about money?" Lucy asked.

"No, I think it's distribution."

"What does that mean?"

Felipe looked out the window, almost disconnected from the conversation, and it was the way his mind worked in deep thought.

"They disputed who to sell to or how the weapons were used," Felipe said. "I've seen it a few times. Davis wants to snitch on Wiggins, and he's got a better offer and more cash for himself."

Lucy paused, thinking of the last conversation with Davis. "The last reach out to me was the guns were being moved."

"That's the hook. Your part is to report Wiggins and the location of the guns."

Lucy sat frustrated. "He'll have no partner and no guns."

Felipe shot back quickly, "No! Wiggins goes to jail, and the ATF only finds a third of the guns. Davis will have moved most of the weapons away before the raid."

"Is Davis not still on the run?"

Felipe went back into his deep thinking. "It's the only way to get rid of the partner and stop the ATF from continuing to search for weapons."

"Oscar Sanchez walks away free?"

"And rich," Felipe said. "I'll bet Oscar Sanchez's name is clean as a whistle. He changed his name when he came to this country and hoped the Feds never find the reputation he left behind. Oscar will always have a clean picture ID and passport ready to flee the country."

Lucy was a little hesitant to offer the location of the guns when asked. However, it was too late to resist Felipe's help with the ATF looking at her as involved. Her hand shook so much writing the address she had to write it twice to read.

"Felipe, the garage on North Rampart Street. Look for a trap door.

"Where? On the floor or wall?"

"I have no clue. I know it's in the garage someplace, and it will lead you down under the house. That's where the guns are stored."

"I'll handle your friends," Felipe said. "And the guns."

A knock at the glass partition interrupted the conversation.

"Excuse me," Darby said as the window went down. "Just got a call from Big Sally, and he said you're set at the warehouse with Mr. Bozzano at nine tomorrow night."

"Holy shit Mama, you came through," Felipe said, opening the door and stepping out.

The statement at that moment made Lucy feel sick to her stomach. She had just sent Big Sally and Bozzano to their death. More than likely—Juan Vargas, too.

CHAPTER 22

Present Day 7:00 a.m.

MARK AND CLARK SAT in a used, jacked-up Jeep with three hundred and seventy-five horsepower at the corner of Magazine Street. The Jeep was delivered overnight by business associates from Alabama. Transported from a used car lot and placed in an enclosed trailer, it arrived at a parking garage downtown.

Professionals in the brothers' line of work had connections. They could get anything from their underground criminal networks for the right price. Using the vehicle would end tonight after they took out their targets and swapped vehicles at the bus station. The car would be left in a tow-away zone to ensure the police identified it as stolen. That would keep the police looking into the bus departures for a few days while they were long gone by air to the islands.

Everything was coming together, and the next step was in place when Clark saw Daniel, the linen truck driver, make his first stop of the day at the Café.

The Jeep pulled around, dropped Clark off at the

linen truck, and parked down the street at Bozzano's warehouse.

"Daniel," Clark said, surprising him when he returned with dirty linens from the Café.

"Agent Thompson," Daniel said, opening the truck's rear door and placing the dirty linen inside.

Clark motioned for Daniel to step behind the truck curbside. "See that Jeep," pointing down the street. "Surveillance is set up." He watched Daniel's reaction, scared yet showing some excitement like he was part of the team.

"I hoped it wouldn't come to this, but a decision was made. The FBI needs your help."

Before Clark could get the entire statement out, Daniel answered, "Sure, how can I help?"

Clark took Daniel back into the coffee shop. They sat for as long as it took for Clark to learn the details of what he would see when he walked inside the kitchen of Bozzano's nightclub and restaurant.

The first question was what linens to take in and if there was a guard inside. Where to place the fresh napkins and tablecloths. Daniel did his part and described every foot through the kitchen into the main dining room. Then he said on the left wall of the dining room there was a large antique armoire with mirrored doors. That's where the fresh linen went.

When Clark learned the details, he asked for Daniel's company vest and truck. He'd make the delivery to the restaurant, and when finished checking out the interior, he'd leave the truck parked on the side street.

"The FBI thanks you, Daniel," Clark said and slipped five one-hundred-dollar bills across the table under a paper napkin.

Daniel's eyes lit up like a Christmas tree, and he slowly lowered the money into his pocket. "I am proud to serve, sir."

Clark walked out of the Café with Daniel's logo vest, putting it on as he walked to the truck. He drove the truck. stopping in the street long enough for Mark to shove a canvas bag through the window. Then he pulled to the side street and parked.

"Can you hear me?" Clark said into a microphone attached to an earpiece.

"Copy," Mark replied. "I'll be in the alley if anything goes sideways."

"I give the word. You come in blasting."

"Hopefully, not," Mark replied. "We only get one shot at this target."

"Yes," Clark said. "Let's make it a bullseye."

Clark pulled a hand cart from the truck and rested it on the ground. Then cut a slit in the plastic, keeping a dozen cloth napkins together. He pulled an automatic weapon from the canvas bag, placing it between the napkins. He repeated the process with three more bundles. The plan for each brother was to have an automatic weapon and a handgun.

"Going in," Clark said and rolled the cart to the alley.

Mark came from the Jeep and stood post at the edge of the building. If needed, he could sprint to the kitchen within seconds.

Clark rolled into the kitchen like he had been there often. He smiled and nodded to the only two people working who were prepping for the day's menu. It was way too early for the bosses to be around. He had the dining room door in view when a voice called out.

"Hey, you!"

Clark stopped and slowly turned around. It put Mark on alert when he replied.

"Sorry, are you talking to me?"

"Yeah, who are you?" a big overweight man said. "Where is Daniel?"

"He's out today. I fill in for vacations, sick days, or Mondays when drivers are nursing a hangover." He wanted to keep Mark in the know, so he talked more than usual since the mic wouldn't pick up what the big guy said.

"I hear that. We get our share of no-shows around here, too," he said. "Come over here."

Clark left the cart and walked toward the man.

In the alley, Mark got closer to the kitchen door.

"My name is Frankie," the big guy said. "No offense, but I don't know you." That's when Frankie frisked Clark.

"Frisk me? What is this? A bank vault?" Clark laughed, but it was mainly for Mark to know he was being detained.

The cart was across the room, and he wasn't packing, so he let Frankie do his thing. A few pats up and down his legs, but it didn't go too low because the big guy would have trouble standing back up.

"Anything serious?"

"Serious?" Clark asked.

"Daniel, anything serious? I know his wife has been sick."

Clark quickly walked to the cart. "Yeah, I heard someone in the family was sick. Maybe he took the day off to help his wife."

"He's a nice family man," Frankie said.

Then he walked to a pot of red sauce cooking on the stove. He lifted the lid and put a spoon in for a taste. "*Cugino!*" he shouted to the prep cook in Italian.

"Yeah, cousin," the man answered.

"Add a tablespoon of cinnamon and a half cup of sugar."

Clark headed to the dining room while Frankie tweaked the sauce.

The layout of the dining room was just like Daniel said. He opened the mirrored doors of the armoire, moved four bundles of tablecloths from the bottom to the top shelves, and placed his four bales on the bottom. There was no way business could be so good in one night that someone would discover the guns before the brothers' ambush of Bozzano and his crew.

Rolling the dirty linen out, he noticed a booth in the center of the room. It was a different leather color and sat more people—maybe eight. It faced the middle of the dance floor. He walked closer to read a sign placed on the tabletop.

Reserved, Clark saw when he got closer to the sign. *Perfect,* he thought. *No doubt that is Bozzano's private booth.*

Clark made his way through the kitchen with the dirty linen. He became invisible to the other employees. He made it to the door and heard the big guy shout out.

"*Voglio che un sandwich di polpette di carne se ne vada?*"

Clark gave a dead stare.

Frankie chuckled. "What, you don't speak Italian?

"Sorry, I don't speak the language."

"Just asked if you want a meatball sandwich to go?" Frankie laughed to a point his big belly shook.

"Too early for such rich food," Clark said.

"Never too early for red sauce," Frankie shot back, biting into a meatball.

Clark fulfilled his mission, placed the dirty linen in the truck, secured the cart, and left the key in the cab. He paced to the Jeep and got in the passenger seat.

"Everything good?" Mark asked.

"Golden," Clark said. "It's going to be an easy job. The guns are in the armoire in the dining room bottom shelf between the linen. After killing our marks, we go out the back. Bozzano's booth is near the kitchen door—much easier exit than the front entrance planned."

CHAPTER 23

Present Day 10:30 a.m.

Lucy roamed around the bedroom. She took three outfits out of the closet and arranged them on the bed. She then swapped one top with the other pants. Her mind was not interested in what to wear. A restless night had her tossing until the sun came up. The night terrors were happening more often as a sign she was under extreme pressure and spiked anxiety. It felt genuine to her, but this time not all the faces were clear.

Bazzano's nightclub was the only vivid part, with dead bodies draped on a table and the floor covered in blood and flesh. Then like most dreams, the scenes jumped. The only person she recognized was Felipe surrounded by guns in Cole Wiggins's house. Then her vision switched back to the restaurant, and Big Sally was on the floor covered in blood. All for revenge with Bozzano.

Now awake and able to evaluate everything, she knew even if she came out of this alive, in time Bozzano would come for her.

She grabbed the jeans and white button-down shirt from the bed and yelled, "Darby!"

"Yeah, Boss?" She answered from the bottom of the stairs.

"Get Stella on the phone. Have her meet in thirty minutes at the coffee shop," Lucy shouted. "I don't care if she's in the middle of a crime scene—just get there."

Lucy dressed and was down the stairs within a few minutes. Darby sat at the front entrance with the SUV motor running.

"All set?" Lucy said, getting in the back seat.

"Yes," Darby replied. "Stella said it better be good. She's up to her eyeballs with paperwork.

The SUV stopped in front of the coffee shop.

"Put your flashers on. This will be quick," Lucy said.

Lucy spotted Stella at a table in the garden area. Two cups of coffee sat ready.

"I like your casual style today," Stella said.

"No time for your flirtatious remarks," Lucy said standing at the table. "I know you like a book. You screwed me over, and now you want to make up with your naughty comments."

"Dammit, Lucy! Lighten up," she shot back.

"Let me make this short. Get the ATF off my ass. I hear things on the street, and I passed it to you to handle. Not for you to shine the light on me."

"I know. Are you going to sit down?"

Lucy took a seat and sipped the coffee. "Information just falls in my lap."

"I know your ear is always to the ground," Stella said. "What is this all about?"

"You want a promotion? Drop this on the ATF," Lucy slipped a note across the table. "North Rampart Street. I don't know how long the guns will be there, but as of this moment, that's the location. Look for a trap door in the garage. That's all I know."

"You're sure?" Stella said, reading the address. "The word I got the weapons are in the old warehouse district behind the potato chip factory."

"You go with what your people think—and the guns will be long gone." Lucy stood and took a sip of coffee. "You don't have much time."

"Time?" Stella's eyebrows went up. "Like a day?"

"More like hours. You put me on the ATF radar. Now be the hero and give them the weapons," she said, pausing. "Just get them off my ass."

CHAPTER 24

Present Day 10:45 a.m.

AFTER AN HOUR OF searching for a utility truck, Mark spotted a New Orleans Electric and Gas company vehicle at the corner of Canal Street.

A man was working on a pole line from the bucket on the back of the truck. Clark stopped next to the truck and Mark stepped out. He jumped into the vehicle that idled and hit a switch. The stabilizers raised, putting the wheels back on the ground, leaving the bucket swinging side to side as the man held on for his life. Then Mark lowered the bucket and the workman jumped before the truck hit a high rate of speed.

Clark met the utility truck a few blocks away, and the two brothers put on blue with red trim jumpsuits with the company logo on the pocket.

Checking the address twice, Mark stopped in front of the residence on North Rampart Street. Clark followed in the Jeep and parked a few houses down.

"Follow my lead," Clark said to his brother, walking up

to the front door with an official company clipboard under his arm.

He knocked at the door hard and fast, and it got an immediate reaction from the homeowner.

"What the hell! What are you banging on my door for!" A man shouted.

"Mr. Cole Wiggins?" Mark said, flashing some sticker he found in the truck. "Sorry, we have a gas leak report in your house."

"Who says? I didn't call anyone."

"It's all computer-generated from your meter," Clark shot back. "Can I check your stove?"

A strange look came over Wiggins's face. Mark got nervous and rested his hand on the gun in his pocket.

"Check my stove? Sure, go ahead," then he whipped out a thirty-eight-revolver waving it at the brothers. "My stove is electric, so why didn't your computer tell you that?"

Clark, a professional, was quick on his feet and was always prepared. "Sir, what about your heater it's gas, not electric, right?"

He then jammed the gun in the back of his belt. "Go head, and hurry."

"Anyone else in the house? They should get close to an exit." Clark said professionally, then stepped down the hall.

"No, my daughter is at school," he replied.

Clark walked through the living room, took a lamp from an end table, and threw it across the room It smashed against the wall, making an ear-splitting crash.

Wiggins took two steps forward, pulling his gun from behind. "What's going on!"

He was not quick enough and took his eyes off Mark in the doorway. Mark put two bullets to the back of Wiggins's head from a Smith & Wesson with a silencer attached.

They left the body in the hallway and headed to the garage. It took about three minutes for the brothers to find the hidden door leading to the guns. Mark backed the Jeep into the garage and pulled three boxes of high-power rifles up the steps. It took both men to lift them into the Jeep.

As directed, Clark surveyed the cellar, leaving one crate of rifles. There were a few handguns, and they sacked them. The front door was locked, and they went out of the garage, pulling the overhead doors down. They followed Felipe's instructions perfectly.

The utility truck was taken a block away from where they stole it and left the keys on the dashboard. It was a clean getaway and far enough from the North Rampart murder to not be associated with it.

Clark wiped the cabin clean and jumped in the Jeep. "The police should classify the murder as a home invasion gone bad," Clark said. Mark agreed, and he drove to the drop-off point.

The Jeep arrived at a warehouse on Royal Street about eight blocks east of the French Quarter. The building was backed up to the river where forklifts unloaded containers of coffee beans. A man met Mark and directed him around the vast warehouse. A forklift loaded the guns into an empty container and placed them into the belly of the ship.

The brothers sat back in the truck and watched the

well-planned caper. The entire robbery took less than thirty minutes.

Mark opened a canvas bag and picked up two bundles of money. "Felipe pays well, and I hate to go on the run and lose out on future paydays."

"Let's get this bag to the bus station locker," Clark said, driving slowly out of the warehouse. "How much cocaine do you think those guns will bring back to Felipe when it hits the Cartel in Columbia?"

"The man does have connections," Clark said. "And powerful friends."

CHAPTER 25

Present Day 3:00 p.m.

It took several hours for Stella to convince her superiors to act on the information she had received earlier that morning. Keeping Lucy's visit earlier that morning out of the conversation, the version she fed to the commander was information overheard by a snitch on the street, easily attained for a twenty-dollar bill. She was warned her career and the commanders were on the line if anything went wrong. She already knew that was a given.

All the law enforcement divisions met in the underground garage of the police station on Tulane Avenue and Broad Street. An enclosed panel truck with blacked-out windows had six ATF agents highly armed, followed by a local police car with two officers leading and a backup unit following. Stella brought up the rear with the commander in the passenger seat.

Stella had stared down the barrel of a gun and had a gun pointed at her. She was shot at often and even had a scar on her thigh from being grazed by a bullet. None of that made her as nervous as sitting next to the commander on their way to make a bust. The total responsibility fell on her shoulders.

Stella thought she knew Lucy, but their relationship had her second-guessing herself. All she knew was Lucy owned a prominent beauty salon in the French Quarter. That alone could not support her clothes, much less the lifestyle. She couldn't pinpoint her involvement or connection to anything illegal, but she didn't rule it out. She blocked the thoughts and went with her gut when coming forward, and now she had to see it through.

Looking at his watch, an officer in the lead car shouted, "It's time!" and waved his arm. Two motorcycle officers jumped in front to control the traffic. One by one, the vehicles popped out of the darkness of the underground garage onto Broad Street. The first motorcycle stopped the traffic, and all the police cars flashed overhead lights going forward. The motorcycles moved up, stopping at traffic lights until they made it three blocks from the North Rampart address. The street was blocked with police vehicles so no traffic could pass.

The ATF agents led with a ramrod in full sprint. Police officers followed with guns extended. They stopped at the door, and the door busted open with one swing of the ram. Police ran in, shouting, *Police--don't move*. Then the room went quiet.

"He's dead," the lead officer said, bending down and checking Cole Wiggins.

When Stella and the commander got inside, the word of Wiggins's dead body had made it to them.

The commander looked at Stella. If she could have melted into the floor, she would have.

"You two come with me," the commander said, pointing to the closest ATF agents. Stella followed. The trap door was left visible for the police to find. It was another point Felipe demanded.

It took seconds for them to open the door, and the two agents stepped down into the cellar. More than enough light from the garage gave them visibility where they found the guns.

One crate of guns was brought to the center of the floor, and the tops were popped open. The commander removed a few and looked at the depth of the stack. "Looks like sixty

Military-grade rifles."

One of the ATF agents picked a rifle up and looked it over. "Commander, I am familiar with these guns."

"Afghanistan?" The commander asked.

"Yes, sir." He spoke. "M2 Browning. This high-power shoots off bullets faster than you can blink, can cut through a twelve-inch brick wall, and still kill its target."

Stella watched from a distance, then stepped closer and made eye contact with the commander. "Are we good?"

He gave a head nod. "Absolutely. No telling where these guns were headed." The commander smiled at Stella. "Good job, Detective. But I expected a lot more guns from an arms dealer."

"Thank you, sir," she replied. "If you like I can get a team together and comb every inch."

"It's your murder case. Go find who did us a favor

and killed that son of a bitch," the commander said and stepped toward the door. "Tossing the house is not a bad idea. Maybe there are more guns."

"I have a good idea," Stella said and reached for her phone. On the second ring, Lucy answered and gave her the information needed. Stella rounded up the ATF and asked them to follow her. The vehicles took off at a high rate of speed until they arrived on Royal Street. Then they crept slowly and parked two doors down from John Davis Fabrics.

The ATF agents swarmed the store finding John Davis. When Stella came in, he was in handcuffs behind his head.

"John Davis or Oscar Sanchez, whatever name you care to use today. "You're under arrest for firearm dealing and the murder of Cole Wiggins."

The ATF won with little resistance from Stella and the Chief of Police when they were told John Davis was booked on Arms Trafficking in a Federal Court. After finding several texts between the two men, it was an easy charge to make stick. One text showed Davis was involved in the purchase and planned to sell the guns. Charging him for murder would have been a long, drawn-out process, so an agreement was made quickly.

Stella made her way back to the Royal Street precinct. The news traveled fast, and the buzz around the office was she had taken down a Colombia Cartel arms dealer. What happened around a building full of cops was usually that the story got successively added to as it was repeated. Fellow officers also questioned how she knew the gun smuggler was sitting in the French Quarter only blocks away.

Stella kept her cool. "That's why I preach to keep your snitches close. They are the ones that have their ears to the ground and can help you bring down criminals."

She walked up the stairs to her office and felt good knowing she was responsible for the takedown. Reaching for a cup of coffee, still lukewarm in the pot, she poured one cup and flopped in her desk chair.

Dialing a number on her cell phone, Darby answered on the second ring.

"Hello, Super Cop," Darby replied. It was something she called Stella when her voice was upbeat, knowing it was difficult joking with a homicide cop.

Darby handed off the phone to Lucy. "Well, are you a hero?" Lucy asked.

"Very much so, thanks to you, and we took down some real bad guys."

"Then that is all that matters. I was happy to do my civil duty. Is my name cleared?"

"I spoke with the ATF and the Commander. They all thank you very much for coming forward. Some high-ranking brass from the uptown precinct called in and talked very highly of you."

"Well, that was nice," Lucy said.

"Do you know a Robert Moreau?" Stella asked.

Lucy shot back quickly and confidently, "No—can't say I do."

"This Moreau guy? The Commander called him "Dutch"—and he said you were the pillar of the community. That he knew you for years."

"Really," Lucy replied. "I can't place him."

"Lucy, this is a big deal for me," Stella said and warmly thanked her. "Let me take you to dinner."

"You're paying?"

"Yes!" Stella shouted.

"Then I want to go to Domenica and have drinks at the Sazerac Bar," Lucy shot back.

"At The Roosevelt? Holy crap, Lucy."

"You wanted to thank me. It's going to cost you."

"Yeah, but I was thinking Bob's Burger Joint."

They laughed, and Stella said she'd reserve time for that night and hung up.

Down the street from the police station, Lucy sat upstairs above Le Salon, sipping a drink in a beautiful living room at Club Twilight. Her phone was handed off to Darby, and she motioned her away.

Staring at a handsome man sitting across from her, she smiled broadly. He was slightly older than she was, but he was worldly. They had talked many nights during his visits to Club Twilight about places he had been which Lucy had only dreamed about. He was a man who made her heart flutter and kept her confused about her sexual preferences.

She leaned over and gave the man a kiss, then he stole a more passionate kiss, and she didn't resist.

"Now really, Dutch?" Lucy said, taking the smear of lipstick off his lips. "Was that the best you could come up with? I'm a pillar of the community?"

"Well, you didn't give me much notice," he said.

CHAPTER 26

Present Day 5:00 p.m.

Lucy sat relaxed in the spa bath at the Lakefront house. The bubbles were high, and the jets hit her back in all the right places. Darby knocked and came in with an Old-Fashioned cocktail and placed it spa-side. Then she took a seat on the vanity chair.

"You know what I have to do tonight," Lucy said.

"We hashed it over many times," Darby replied with a slight exhale. "It may not be today, but someday Bozzano will give the order. When he no longer needs you, he'll order you dead."

Lucy shook her head. It wasn't anything she didn't know. Washing Bozzano's gambling money and knowing too much about his business made her realize that unless you're the top dog and the pack leader, you're dead when they have no more use for you.

She and Darby talked many nights. It was time for her to go legit. There was only one way to make that happen. Kill off Bozzano and Felipe. The drug business would stop cold in the City of New Orleans. No dealer to bring the product to the city, no big man to finance illegal activity, and the street rats would move on someplace else.

Add a third person and takedown: Juan Vargas. That would stop other dealers from coming into the city when they saw the others had fallen.

To pull off all three was wishful thinking, that's why she designed the plan they were going with tonight. Nobody died, hopefully, and things would run smooth for many years, and maybe someday soon Bozzano would die of natural causes.

"What time do we have to leave?" Darby asked.

"About an hour and a half," Lucy said.

"Do you know what you're going to tell Bozzano?"

"Not sure," Lucy said. "You're a real buzzkill." Holding her glass up like she was at a bar for another.

Darby took the glass, headed downstairs, stopped midway, turned, and ran back to the bathroom.

"Lucy!" She shouted.

Scaring the hell out of her, she snapped. "What!"

Darby's eyes widened. "Remember when you asked me to follow Cole Wiggins for a few days and see who he associated with and his regular stops."

"Yeah, so what?" Lucy said, reaching for a towel on the rack and covering herself.

"One of his stops was the daughter's school. She sat waiting on a bench across the street, waiting for Cole to pick her up."

Lucy saw the look in Darby's eyes. Her heart sank, thinking how often her father, Edgar, forgot to pick her up from school because he was drunk in a bar or running some scam that took longer than expected. Either way, she sat until dark, waiting until Wanda sent a neighbor out for her.

"Darby, there is no mother, and neither the ATF nor Stella know the child exists."

Darby darted out of the house without a word and jumped into Baby, her black and yellow 1957 Chevrolet convertible with 283 HP. The engine roared in the garage as she pulled out, and hitting the street, the tires did their best to grip the ground. The engine was too strong, and the tail shifted side to side until Darby straightened the wheel. She raced to the school, running some traffic lights, not caring about cops stopping her. Baby could outrun any car on the street.

She slowed down at the empty parking lot, except for a janitorial vehicle with two men unloading cleaning equipment. Across the street Darby spotted Beth on a bench doing homework.

"Hi Beth, I am Darby," she said, taking a seat next to her.

Beth looked up, and her face dripped with tears.

"Your Dad sent me to pick you up," Darby said, doing her best to make the child feel comfortable. She mentioned the North Rampart Street house and how she knew her father, further creating more lies about how she knew Beth and Jane Davis were friends.

"Come on, I have a place you can spend the night. Your Dad is going to be late tonight." Gathering up her knapsack, she got Beth in the car and drove.

Darby did what she thought a parent would do on the way. "How was school today?"

NIGHT TERRORS

There was no answer from the child, whose face turned scared.

"Are you okay?" Darby asked. "I promise nothing is going to happen to you. I was told to take you to a place where some women live, and they will feed you and help with your homework until Dad picks you up."

The car stopped at the Burdette house and Beth was walked to the front entrance. One knock and a lady opened the door. Darby asked for Wanda, and she was escorted to her office.

"Hi Wanda, Lucy asked if you could look after little Beth, just for a few hours?"

"Of course, hi Beth. I am Ms. Wanda," she said, patting the back of Beth's head.

Giving Beth a kiss on the cheek, she shifted her eyes Wanda's way, giving a nod. Wanda never asked questions and just followed through when asked.

"Ms. Darby," Beth said quitely.

"Yes?" She replied.

"It's okay. My Dad left me before and didn't return for two years, I lived with a friend, and then the city took me to foster care. I'm ten years old now, and I understand. He's not coming back, and he's in jail or dead."

Darby couldn't answer. Her throat had such a lump it stopped her from speaking.

"Come along, Beth. I bet you're hungry," Wanda said, directing Beth to the kitchen.

"Thanks, Wanda," a sad-faced Darby tried to muster up a smile. "Beth, I'll come by later."

"I'll take care of everything, Darby." Wanda moved

the child along, and she was welcomed by the ladies in the kitchen.

CHAPTER 27

Present Day 7:00 p.m.

Darby filled Lucy in on Beth's rescue. Her quick thinking may have saved the child's life from being tossed from foster homes until she was eighteen years old.

"The Burdette House is the safest place for the child," Lucy said, praising Darby's quickness in the rescue.

"Lucy?" Darby said, looking back at her in the back seat. "This kid has no one. She's been in foster care before, and I don't think it was a good experience."

"Never is," Lucy shot back. "She stays with Wanda until I can figure things out. Besides, no one knows she exists."

The car pulled curbside at the entrance of Bozzano's Dinner Club. She didn't think she was overdressed with a short skirt, silk blouse, and a flashy waistcoat—until she saw women walking in with jeans and sheer tops.

"You look great," Darby said. "Good luck and be strong."

Lucy gave a weak smile. "I am nervous as hell."

Inside, Lucy was met by Big Sally, and he escorted her directly to Bozzano's booth. Putting on her best smile she walked straight back on her heels, but her guts were shaking. There were no less than four bodyguards near the private area, and that was just the men she spotted. Sure, there were more, maybe sitting as couples at tables near the boss. One man ate with a woman, but his eyes were locked on Bozzano when she took a seat.

"Mr. Bozzano," Lucy said, extending her hand.

Tony stood and welcomed her with a handshake and a kiss.

It was a good start. The first gentlemanly gesture she'd seen from this creep of a monster.

A waiter brought an antipasto platter and poured red wine for two. They sat and made small talk for a minute, then Lucy cut it off. It was no time for Bozzano's boring childhood stories dating back to the old country.

She watched everyone nervously as they passed. Sitting in public with the man people around town knew as the "Mafia Boss" made her uncomfortable. She still didn't know what to tell Bozzano. After asking Big Sally for a sit-down, she had not come up with a reason to meet. Knowing the specific time Bozzano would be in the club was accomplished. She toyed with several things to say but her heart wanted to shout out: *Felipe will kill you.*

Lucy second-guessed herself and could have easily been a no-show. But if anything went wrong, all eyes would be on her for getting the mafia boss to the club an hour earlier.

She watched Bozzano load antipasto on a chunk of Italian bread, then stuff the entire piece into his mouth. The olive oil dripped down his chin as he chewed like she remembered seeing a cow eat once. His tongue came out, yet he chewed.

You disgusting ass ran through her mind. Today she had to play nice.

"So, sweetheart," Bozzano said, tapping her hand.

When the chills stopped running down her spine from a mere touch of the creep, she blurted out. "I don't know if you heard of my psychic tendencies. I have dreams that often come true."

"And what does that mean?"

Lucy had to follow up with an answer, and a dream was a good reason to ask for a meeting. All though she had never seen him in her dreams, she immediately made one up.

"Take this for what it's worth," Lucy said, staring into his eyes. Something she heard he hated. "Someone is trying to kill you."

Bozzano gave a belly laugh, "Oh, honey! Tell me something I don't know. Why do you think I have a half dozen bodyguards?"

She had to keep the charade going, but she wasn't sure how. She reached for a piece of bread and put a spoon full of olives and peppers on the plate, which allowed her time to think.

"That's my point in the dream. It's someone close to you, a person you trust."

"One of my bodyguards?" Bozzano asked, looking around the room and stopping at each man he paid to protect him and his family. It didn't take long for him to get agitated. Bozzano went from zero to a hundred in seconds on the emotional scale.

"Who?"

"I don't know for sure," Lucy said.

Tony pounded the table, spilling olive oil and peppers. "You don't come to me with this kind of half-ass information."

Lucy's heart raced. *What have I got myself into?* She thought. One thing for sure, she had to fix it quick. Taking control, she reached for his hand even though it repulsed her.

"It's my night terrors. I've had them for years, but I believe—" A clearer picture came to Lucy. Bozzano trusted her washing his money, his secret of how he earned the illegal cash, and how she passed it back to him. She gambled at putting Juan and Tony at odds.

"Just maybe Juan is coming to you with intentions of taking over the drug business when what he really wants is your empire. Really, Tony," she said, patting his hand again. "You know how things work. Juan gets closer to you to learn, then he cuts you out of the drugs, gambling, and prostitution."

"Maybe his promises," Tony paused giving her a side glance. "Are nothing but bullshit."

"Tony, it's a dream," she said. "But some have come true, and I felt I had to warn you."

Tony Bozzano wasn't a man of compassion or at least with people outside his family. He gave her a stern look as if he was studying her. It frightened Lucy at first.

"Never be afraid to come to me with a dream or what you hear on the street," he said. "You did good by coming forward. Juan came out of nowhere but with strong references from people I thought I could trust. Maybe I should be more careful. I'm not as young as when I got into this business. Maybe I am too trusting. Thank you."

Lucy mustered up her best smile, shook his hand, and slipped out of the booth. She hit the front door in a flash and found the car parked across the street. Before Darby could open the door, Lucy did it herself and jumped in the back seat.

"Drive!" She shouted.

Lucy laid her head on the headrest and took a deep breath. *What have I done?*

"Where to?" Darby asked.

"Just drive!"

CHAPTER 28

Present Day 9:00 p.m.

Mark and Clark stopped the Jeep in front of the warehouse. The place looked different than it did earlier that morning. Sounds of cars moving through the valet line echoed through the street. A doorman greeted the ladies decked out in their best and most revealing outfits. As they stepped on the red doormat runner delivered that morning, it was like a premiere. The ladies smiled, strutting as they passed the doorman holding the red velvet rope open.

After careful deliberation, the brothers decided a separate getaway driver was too risky. Taking out three men at once would be the biggest job they had ever attempted, and it was best not to involve an outsider. The only people they could count on were each other.

The Jeep was parked on the street near the entrance of the kitchen. The plan was for Mark to take Bozzano, Big Sally, and Juan Vargas down. Clark's job was to spray bullets at the bodyguards from an automatic weapon. It should take twelve seconds, which they timed at a makeshift farm, repeatedly practicing until they got it within the right window of seconds needed. They would rush through the kitchen at completion, continuing to shoot randomly so the staff would hit the floor as they exited. If it went well, they should be in the Jeep within twenty-one seconds of the first shot being fired.

The two well-dressed men walked from the Jeep and stopped at the door. After a deep breath, Mark looked at Clark and said, "Let's do it."

Mark gave Johnny Russo's name to the doorman with a pleasant smile, and they were sent to the podium. While neither looked Italian, using Russo's name helped them blend in, but most of all, it got them a reservation when they wanted. At the stand, the man with the tuxedo looked his board over for a table for two, and Mark's hand came under the edge and slipped the man a one-hundred-dollar bill.

"We want to be close to the dance floor," Mark said. "You know we came for the food… but for the ladies, too."

The man glanced at the money. His eyes widened, and with a smile, he said. "Absolutely, follow me, Mr. Russo."

He stopped at a table, and Mark motioned to another he had scouted out, which would put them in front of the armoire and directly to the side of Bozzano's table. They were told the table was reserved and took a seat on the chair the man pulled out. They were at the edge of the dance floor and only a few steps from the guns in the armoire.

"This will work," Mark said to his brother. "I'm sure that table is for Bozzano's goons."

"Not a problem," Clark shot back. "They will be the first to go down."

They ordered wine, picking one of the most expensive labeled on the menu as a *Reserve* bottle priced at two hundred and thirty dollars. The wine was delivered in a silver bucket with no ice, and the waiter recommended a slight chill for the best taste.

Two glasses were poured, then the waiter backed away from the table. The brothers raised their glasses.

"To a successful night," Mark said.

They sipped. "Wow, this is good for overpriced wine," Clark said. "But then again, we're not paying the bill."

"Showtime!" Mark whispered. His eyes shifted to what was the empty table. Two men sat down, and they were undoubtedly part of Bozzano's crew. The bulge in their coats showed they were packing guns.

A four-piece band played dinner music, and a few couples took to the floor. The lights dimmed, and the mood was set as a romantic dinner restaurant.

Mark had a perfect view of the double doors leading from the kitchen, and he tapped the table with three fingers spread. "Bozzano is in the house," he said.

Tony's men did a room glance before allowing the boss to walk to his table, and big Sally followed up the rear and sat.

Clark spotted Juan at the podium. "The party is about to start."

The tuxedoed man passed just behind the brother's table with Juan Vargas. Before sitting, he reached for Tony's hand, placing his other hand on Tony's forearm, giving a hearty handshake.

Clark focused on a waiter that opened the armoire doors. He spotted the lumps in the tablecloths on the bottom shelf where he stashed the guns.

"Everything is still in place," Clark said.

"Then we are a go," his brother replied.

Clark ran down the process again. "Bottom shelf right side: two handguns. Left: the AK's. Use the pistol at close range for the thugs. I'll spray the ceiling and get people screaming. You'll manage the three in the booth."

"You're, okay?" Mark asked.

"I'm good. We can plan all we want at the farm," Clark said. "But this is the dress rehearsal."

When the food was served to Bozzano, they would make their move. If they were lucky, the bodyguards would eat simultaneously. All they wanted was a split second for them to be distracted.

From Bozzano's booth, loud laughter came. Mark glimpsed what looked like Tony telling a story.

Then a waiter rolled a cart to the front of the booth. He lit a burner and dropped bacon pieces in a pan, then drizzled sherry, adding garlic and herbs, the scents of each noticed from a distance.

"Smells good," Clark said.

"Have to give Bozzano a good last meal," Mark said, laughing it off.

Then fresh Spinach was mixed into the heated bacon grease and covered with brown sugar, taking the aroma to the next level.

Clark poured another glass of wine for both. "When the cart moves from Bozzano's table, we take action."

His brother gave nod. "That guy at the kitchen door keeps looking at us."

"Yeah, I see him," Clark said. "I saw him downstairs in the casino a few nights ago when we scouted the place out. Someone called him Richie. He must be a do-all for Bozzano—casino, kitchen, backup goon."

"I'll plant a clip into the thin metal doors," Mark said. "He'll either have to run for cover or be dead when we start shooting the place up."

Richie surfaced again and went directly to Bozzano like he was summoned. The two talked briefly, then Richie returned to the kitchen.

"Something is up," Clark said. "Not sure I like this. We might have to move our timeline up." Before Clark could get another word out, Richie came back out from the kitchen, and next to him standing was Daniel.

"The linen truck driver?" Mark said.

Richie spoke in Daniel's ear. Daniel gave a nod up and down.

From that point, things happened quickly. The next thing Mark and Clark heard was a gun hammer clicking behind their heads.

"Gentlemen," a voice said. "Stand and walk to the kitchen. You make one move, and I'll ruin Mr. Bozzano's meal and all his white tablecloths around the area."

Clark gave a side glance to his brother, and they followed directions. They marched through the kitchen and out the back door.

Daniel was told to get a closer look at Mark and Clark.

"I don't know this one," he said, pointing to Mark.

"The other one identified himself as Agent Thompson with the FBI." Then he got into Clark's face. "The leather wallet you flashed at me was genuine, but the badge was a fake and a terrible copy. I did five years for fraud and could have made a better copy in the dark."

Daniel reached in his pocket and tossed bullets on the ground and three clips. "I wish Mr. B would have let you get to the guns, and I would love to have seen your faces—whipping out guns with no bullets."

Mark and Clark were pinned into a corner, and one man holstered his handgun, pulled an AK-40 from around him, and pointed them to their knees. "Who sent you?" There was no answer.

Richie bent down to eye level with Clark. "What's your name? Your real name?"

Clark didn't answer. He stared him down.

"Look," Richie said. "I can save your life—maybe you'll limp for the rest of your days. Just tell me, who sent you?"

Again, there was no answer.

A beeping sound echoed as one of the men directed a truck backing up. "That's good!" the man shouted.

"Where the hell did Mr. B get a school bus?" The man directing asked Richie.

"Who knows?" Richie said. "He's got connections for anything you need."

Richie returned to Bozzano's table as the waiter removed the Spinach plates.

"Boss," Richie said. "Daniel did good."

Without saying a word, Bozzano shifted a side glance to Big Sally. Sally slipped out of the booth and stepped to Juan.

Juan quickly looked across the room for his men only to see the two being escorted to the kitchen.

Juan's face dropped. He then felt the cold steel gun barrel to his neck.

"Didn't think we knew you'll come with muscle? Let's go," Sally demanded.

"Tony!" Juan, said in powerful whisper. "We had a deal," he said, pleading.

Tony smiled. "An angel came to me. Call it a vision."

"Please, Tony?" He pleaded as he was escorted out through the kitchen.

Big Sally returned to Bozzano's table with Daniel. The young man was openly nervous.

"Come sit down," Bozzano said. "You like mussels and marinara sauce?"

Daniel barely nodded his head. "Yes, sir."

Bozzano gave a nod to the waiter assigned to stand tableside for him. He returned shortly with a platter of mussels on fresh pasta, drowned in red sauce. Dinner plates were placed in front of the men, and the waiter served the food homestyle.

"*Mangiare*," Bozzano said in his native tongue.

As Daniel felt more comfortable, he relaxed and ate.

"How long have you worked for me, Daniel?" Bozzano asked.

"Close to three years," he said. "My lucky day was when I walked out of prison, and you had a car waiting for me. All my worries went away, just like you said. You even got me a job with the linen company. What more could I ask."

"The linen delivery is one of my legit companies.

Getting you a job was easy." He slipped a thick envelope to Daniel. "I need smart people working for me. And you? My friend," he paused, giving Daniel a pinch on his cheek. "Smart move catching the bogus badge and then chasing down the guns in the armoire. Loyalty is important," he said, opening the envelope so Daniel could see the cash.

"Mr. B, you're too generous," Daniel said.

"It's ten G's. There is no doubt you saved my life, and you earned it."

Richie interrupted, standing at the table. His shirt sleeves were rolled up, and he had bloody knuckles, nursing the one hand with an ice pack.

"Mr. B, they didn't give it up easy," Richie said. "Felipe Cruz ordered the hit."

"That ballsy prick," Bozzano said.

"What about the five in the alley?"

Bozzano's nose flared, and he took a second to respond. "Put them all in the bus!"

CHAPTER 29

Present Day 10:00 p.m. Domenica Restaurant

Lucy and Stella had dinner and preferred to stay in the restaurant for after-dinner drinks. Admitting the Sazerac Bar was too crowded—or else they were getting too old to hang with the younger crowd. They both worked on their second Old Fashioned, preferring the Rye Whiskey the Sazerac cocktail is made with.

The night had gone well, and no talk of Stella's work, especially the arrest of John Davis and the murder of Cole Wiggins. She preferred those two be left out of the conversation for tonight, and they were until Stella popped a question.

"By the way, during the search at Cole Wiggins's house, we came across a teenager's bedroom. Some boy band posters on the wall, female clothes in the closet."

Lucy did her best to divert the question. "So what are you getting at?"

"Do you know if Cole had a daughter?"

Lucy's eyes shifted around the room, as she did when her anxiety spiked. "I had a few conversations with him."

Then she put on a stern face. "Can't say I know of a daughter."

"I know he's renting the house by the week," Stella said. "So, it might be something the owner left."

"Yeah, probably so," Lucy shot back an unconcerned tone.

It was a perfect distraction to get Stella off the subject when the waiter placed the leather holder in the center of the table with the bill. Lucy reached for it, and Stella's hand got to it first.

"Don't make me pull my gun," she said. "I invited you."

"Yeah, but I picked this overpriced place," Lucy said.

Stella would not hear of it and opened the leather cover and viewed the bill. She tried to hide her reaction, but Lucy picked up on it.

"When you put your eyeballs back in your head," Lucy said. "Let's split the bill."

"No, I got it," she said. "I wonder if they take terms?" She laughed. "Dammit, this place is overpriced." Then pulled a credit card from her purse and handed the folder to the waiter.

Taking her phone from the purse, Stella looked at the screen. "Three missed calls."

"I am proud of you," Lucy said. "It was an actual date and no emergency calls."

"I had the ringer off."

"Well, aren't you learning," Lucy said with a snicker. "Off duty, and you turn your phone off. Wow, that's a first."

"Oh crap," Stella said, thumbing through the missed calls. "It was the commander that called—three times."

Lucy motioned with her hand. "Go ahead, call him back. I'll sit and sip my drink alone," making a sad face.

"I'm off tonight but never off duty. I am head of the Detective Division for a reason."

"So, they can call you at any time?" Lucy shot back. "Isn't that right, Super Cop." Lucy knew that bothered Stella then broke a smile.

"I'm going to Super Cop you," Stella said through her teeth.

After their banter, Stella connected with her Commander and got a mouth full. "Yes, sir. Are you sure it's a homicide?" She listened and tried not to let her emotions show. "I'm on my way, sir, tops ten minutes."

Stella stuffed the phone in her purse, then reached back and turned the ringer on. "Lucy, I am sorry."

The waiter delivered the folder, she signed the bill and left a sizeable tip. "Thank you, everything was great."

Turning back to Lucy she said. "Honey, I'm sorry to end it abruptly, but something serious just broke. Well, it's been going on for an hour, but the commander couldn't get in contact with me."

"Anything you can tell me?"

"Only that a school bus went over the wall at the lakefront," Stella said.

"Isn't that an accident? Why are they calling you?"

Lucy wasn't too concerned if they had found five bodies with single shots to the head, she'd know who was involved.

"The street is fifty feet from the road," Lucy said. "How does a bus run over the grass down twenty concrete steps in the lake? And what the hell is a bus doing out this late?"

"It looks like the driver bailed before the bus hit the water."

"So, the driver jumped and saved his ass," Lucy said.

"The diver crew just got to the bottom of the lake. Five men are chained to the bus seats," she said. "I have five bodies."

Lucy's stomach turned when she pictured Tony Bozzano as one body. She and Stella hugged it out, and that quick, their date had ended. Lucy sat and took the last few sips of her cocktail. She then spotted Darby coming in the door with her cell phone in hand, waving it over her head.

"Lucy! You need to take this call."

Taking the phone hesitantly. "Hello?"

"Your night terrors?' He paused. "Were a bullseye. A well-planned hit on me got defused, and now they are dead."

"It was a dream I felt I had to tell you."

"A dream? Were you covering your ass because you knew Felipe ordered me dead?"

"Felipe! Tony, come on," Lucy said nervously. "If I were involved, why would I tell you? Besides, think about it. Why would I want to stop my money train? I'll lose over a million dollars a year, washing your casino money."

There was a long pause. "That's the part I can't figure out," Tony said. "You didn't make your money by being stupid and knocking me off would be real stupid—on your part."

"You have that part correct, Tony. I've made millions off you. Who would kill their golden goose?" Lucy spit out random things to convince him. She'd seen his actions, and Bozzano was seconds away from ordering her dead.

"You get a pass, Lucy, because I am unsure."

Her heart skipped a beat.

"But then again, I have killed before just on suspicion. I don't like taking chances."

"Tony? Please, what can I say to convince you I was not involved?" Lucy said it but knew he could never be trusted.

Play nice, Lucinda said in Lucy's mind. When the time is right, we will kill this murdering bastard.

"As I said, you get a pass," Bozzano whispered, then quickly demanded: "Now find Felipe and give me his location."

Taking a deep breath, she replied with no game plan. "Sure, I'll have the location first thing in the morning."

"And Lucy. If you tip Felipe off—you're dead.

The phone went silent.

Lucy dropped the phone in her purse. With a pleasant smile, she gave a nod to the man at the podium and strutted out with Darby at her heels.

In the SUV, Lucy directed Darby to Felipe's house and then called his cell number. "Come on, Felipe! Answer."

CHAPTER 30

Present Day 11:00 p.m.

DARBY FOLLOWED ORDERS AND drove to Felipe's home on Touro Street. It was all Darby had to hear when Lucy shouted out the order: *I don't care how fast. Just get there quickly.*

Unsuccessfully contacting Felipe, the cell phone sat in her hand. Four attempts went to voice mail, and then she received a returned call. Her phone screen lit up and vibrated.

"Felipe? Where are you?" She listened while he preached that he doesn't like to talk business this late. From the noise in the background, she could hear the resounding beat of a drum. No doubt he was partying at his club with his crew.

"Pull to the curb and stop," she shouted to Darby in the front seat, and she did so immediately.

"Felipe, listen to me," Lucy shouted. "You are in danger, and I mean grave danger if you don't get out of town."

Since she could hear him much better, Felipe must have moved to a quieter area, maybe a bathroom or closet, she thought.

"Get MC on the phone," she heard Felipe directing someone.

"MC?" Lucy asked.

"Hold up, Mama," he replied.

Then Lucy heard through the phone someone tell Felipe. "They don't answer."

"Who is MC?" She asked.

"Mark and Clark," he replied.

Lucy took a deep breath, "Felipe, you tried to kill Bozzano? Why, I could have worked things out…"

"For how long? Remember he's the one that tried to kill me in prison," Felipe shouted. "An eye for an eye."

"I think your MC hit went bad."

"What do you mean?"

"I am pretty sure they are dead at the bottom of the lake, chained to the floor of a bus."

"It—went—south?" Felipe slowly said.

"Very much so, and I think Juan Vargas is with them."

"That old bastard cleaned house," Felipe said. "I'll take him out myself. Personally, I'll watch him die, and it will be in front of his wife and daughter."

"Felipe, if you ever listened to me—pay attention now," she said. "We must get you out of town and now."

"No, Mama, Felipe, don't run from thugs. I'll face Mr. Tony Bozzano eye to eye and spit on him when I take him out."

Darby pulled the car from the curb. She heard from the one-sided conversation they were heading to Burdette House.

Lucy hung up with Felipe and made another call.

NIGHT TERRORS

Wanda answered on the second ring, "Lucy, who died?" It was her usual question when awakened from a deep sleep.

Lucy offered no explanation and directed her to have the rear gates and security waiting in the motor pool area of the Burdette House.

Clicking the phone off, Lucy laid her head back in the seat. She wasn't sure how Felipe was convinced to meet her, but he did agree. She had minutes to develop an exit plan for Felipe. Tony Bozzano would not stop tracking Felipe down until he was dead. Even if Tony was killed, the mob would send another assassin to kill Felipe. It would never stop until the drug dealer who ordered a hit on the mafia's top man had paid for his actions. This would start a war in the streets of New Orleans, and it would get bloody, and a lot of bodies would be left behind.

In the motor pool area stood three men from house security. They directed Darby to the covered area, and soon after, two more SUVs rolled up.

Inside the Burdette House, Wanda had to of the cooks wrestled out of bed to prepare coffee and food for the men. Lucy met in Wanda's office one on one with Felipe.

Lucy explained the little she knew of the massacre. Then she bashed Felipe for ordering the hit on Bozzano. They threw out speculations of how it all went down but the only person that could offer details, and it was a slim shot, was Big Sally.

Lucy said she'd pump Stella on the details of how the men came to their death other than knowing they all drowned. There may have been bullets to Mark and Clark's heads, but Bozzano may have wanted to think about the horror in their face as they slowly struggled with the chains before drowning.

Felipe shot that theory down quickly, thinking like a vicious person.

"Someone takes a shot at me?" He spoke. "They don't get one to the back of the head. No need to submerge the bus. No, Tony wanted them to suffer. They were chained to the floor for a reason, and the dead watched the water inch over their nose. He wanted them to fight the chains to their death and send a message to anyone considering another attempt."

Lucy said, "Come in," When a knock came at the door.

Wanda followed a kitchen lady into the room who pushed a cart with coffee, tea, finger sandwiches, and fruit. They left the cart, and they closed the door behind them.

Felipe, who ate with anxiety, picked through the fruit and then stuffed two finger sandwiches in his mouth.

"If I take Big Sally and Tony out, how many do you think will come after me?" Felipe asked. "That is if they know I did it."

"Felipe, if Tony gets hit by lightning, the New York boss will blame you. There is no way to get out of this," she paused. "You must disappear. We must leave a trail, so they know you ran, but it must be a misdirect."

"Bullshit! Felipe, don't run."

Lucy poured a cup of tea and sat on the sofa across from Felipe. Her silence showed she was thinking and then laid out a plan. The first misdirect was for Felipe to buy a bus ticket to Florida. Right before loading, they'd drop some cash on the driver—enough for him to swear to anyone that Felipe did depart New Orleans to Florida.

Lucy's eyes shifted more than her smile broadened. "We do the same thing at the main airport, and I have a connection who can handle the manifest. It will be easy to put your name on the flight even though you didn't board."

Another knock came at the door, and it opened, and one of Felipe's men dropped a duffel bag on the floor. "It's all there," the man said. "The brothers had not moved the money yet. A few bucks to a security guard who we found asleep at his post, and we took a crowbar to the locker."

"So, the brothers are dead, and I got my money back," Felipe said. "All good."

"No, Felipe, it's far from all good. By 9 A.M., I must give Bozzano your whereabouts, and by noon you'll be dead."

The last piece of the misdirect was Darby would take Felipe in a car to the private jet airport in New Orleans—a hired jet to the islands and a different plane to his destination.

"You'll have tons of cash to start a new life." Lucy explained.

"And my wife and son?" Felipe said.

"They did without you in prison," Lucy said, staring at him. "Give it a year, let things cool down here, and they can follow."

Felipe stretched back in the chair. "I don't think that is going to work for me."

"Dead in a box? Is that what you want?" Lucy stood. "Felipe, you don't have time or choices. We must move quickly."

In Lucy's mind, she had two options. Felipe had to disappear without a trace and hope Tony Bozzano would give up in time. The other option was to put a bullet in Felipe's head, a mercenary killing that was less painful than what Bozzano would do.

How long before Mr. Mob Boss blames Felipe's disappearance on you? Lucinda took control of Lucy's mind.

It was essential to control her anxiety, the doctor preached. Still, Lucy never liked taking the medication prescribed. Her stress point hit the max allowing the devil herself to surface.

Lucy wandered the office, repeating, "The world is a pretty safe place." A reference the doctor gave her when her mind spun out of control.

"Get out, Lucinda!" She shouted and dropped to the floor, her hands over her ears.

"Lucy?" Felipe said. His eyes widened in disbelief.

You said it.

"I said what, Lucinda?"

Kill him yourself.

"No!" Lucy shouted, rolling on the floor. The one time she prayed, doctors were right that only she could hear Lucinda.

"Mama? What the hell is going on?" Felipe stood and moved closer to the door. "Who are you talking to?"

Lucy, think about it, and it would be the ultimate misdirect.

"What are you talking about? A misdirect?" That split second gave her something to think about, and her mind shifted. A calmness came over her.

As fast as the auditory hallucination was heard, it

stopped. Then Lucy picked herself up from the floor and brushed her clothes off, and a slight smile came to her face.

"What the hell, Lucy! I don't like that Voodoo stuff," Felipe said, turning the doorknob.

"Sit down, Felipe," she said as her smile broadened. "I have the ultimate misdirect, and no one will ever come looking for you."

She leaned back and looked at the ceiling, flopping on the desk chair. "Thank you, Lucinda."

CHAPTER 31

THE NEXT DAY LUCY got out of bed after a restless night of virtually no sleep. Her bedroom window with a slight blow from the streetlight in front of her Lakefront home clicked off, and that told her it was a little after five in the morning. Still too early to make the phone calls she decided on the night before, instead she called Darby.

"Are you up?" Lucy said when she answered.

"I am now," she said. "Are you ready for coffee?"

Lucy didn't answer and jumped into the shower. Hot water beat on her back from three directions. She mulled over the plan and could only hope Felipe was one hundred percent on board. He said in time, Bozzano would gun him down or, worse, kidnap his son, then his wife, and leave him for last. Maybe even kill them in front of him.

Felipe was a hardened criminal who was smart enough to know that his life span was short-lived, just like his father, uncle, and cousins. It was the nature of the drug business.

Unlike Tony Bozzano, with protection from coast to coast with the mafia's top man, no one looked to take his position because they feared the people higher up.

Felipe was a drug dealer who made an example of people who crossed him. He found greed overshadowed loyalty, and there was too much cash his people handled daily.

Lucy clarified it to Felipe that *the mob never gives up. They will hunt you down no matter how many you kill—they will never stop looking for you until you're in the ground.*

Lucy shut the water off and grabbed one of the fluffy towels. She wiped the foggy mirror and stared. *You must have done some high talking to get Felipe to leave town.*

In the kitchen, over a cup of coffee, Darby asked. "Has the plan changed?"

"Not that I know of," She replied. "It's Felipe's only option."

Sipping her coffee, Lucy looked out at the yard. The green grass was manicured, the bushes trimmed. A waterfall emptied into the swimming pool.

"You know we need to take advantage of the good weather," Lucy stood and got a better look. "Spend the day at the pool. Maybe treat the girls from the Burdette House and have them come for a cookout and enjoy the place."

"Hello!" Darby shouted, waving her hands. "Who are you, and what did you do with Lucy?"

They both laughed.

"Really, something has to change," Lucy said and sipped her coffee. "I get out of this—alive, and I'm out of the drug business."

"That would eliminate ninety percent of your problems," Darby said. "What about Bozzano's casino money."

"In time, I'll connect him directly with how I funnel his money and the main man in Panama. He's all about making more money, and I'll set him up with my connections."

"Sounds like a plan, but one question," Darby asked, looking at the floor. "Are you okay without Bozzano and Felipe's money funneling in by the truckloads?"

"If you're asking, is my lifestyle going to change?" Lucy said, giving a dead stare. "I have a ton of cash for an emergency and many legit revenue streams monthly. It's more money I ever expected to gather when I first moved to New Orleans. At some point, you must get out or get caught. I like fine things, good restaurants, and lavish parties, and it's time to go fully legit."

Darby peeked up at the sun rising over the clouds, "The sun is up, and first things first, you need to make the calls we talked about last night."

The clock was ticking, and Bozzano expected answers to Felipe's whereabouts before noon. How she handled the next few hours would determine if she lived through the night.

Deep in the closet, behind formal evening dresses draped to the floor, Lucy reached between them for the handle of a combination safe. Spinning the numbers correctly the first time, she pulled the lever down, opening the door. A notebook she called her bible sat among deep stacks of cash and jewelry. The black book was a window into Lucy's good and evil life. Each name spelled out how she did them a favor or how they helped her. Some names even stretched back before she owned the business, but their debt remained with Club Twilight.

NIGHT TERRORS

Vivian made sure of that calling each one before Lucy took over.

Standing for better light, she thumbed through the book pages in the bedroom. The information was in no order other than the date entered. Data was written as things happened over the years. Lucy wrote no one name in the book unless she was indebted to them and willing to return a favor if asked. Still, one thing for sure, there were more people Lucy had performed services for, just for the asking, with a catch. She could call on them to return a favor, and today two men would get the call.

The night before, Lucy ran through her mind a plan and how the men would play a part. The two most qualified to pull off this misdirect were Ben Anderson, a New Orleans Homicide Detective, and Azariah Weber, a Medical Examiner for the Coroner's Office.

Lucy wrote detailed notes, something Vivian Bluff demanded when Lucy took over Club Twilight. Flopping on the bed, she read up on how she helped Ben Anderson. It was a crucial part Vivian preached should she go calling in favors and get refused.

A hit and run-on Canal Street was the call Ben got one Saturday afternoon. He gave resistance, as it did not actually fall under a homicide case. The Police Sargent on the scene strongly suggested he come. On arrival, the officer on duty detailed what people witnessed: a car swerving and running through a red light, hitting a woman. The officer clocked off forty-seven feet as they walked to a body covered in the street with a white sheet. The officer hoped he was wrong but thought the woman was his mother. Ben peeked under the sheet and confirmed.

A year later, Lucy heard the story of a detective looking for revenge for the court's failure to follow through with his mother's justice. Twice charged with driving drunk, the man with deep pockets who killed Ben's mother got the best defense lawyers, and his sentence was reduced to time served.

Two months later, he walked out of a bar, stone drunk. He got behind the wheel of his car and came face to face with a gun. Forced to slide over, and too drunk to fight back, he passed out in the passenger seat. The car was driven to a boat launch where the driver speedily went down the ramp and jumped out right before the car hit the water. His partner picked him up in time to watch the vehicle submerge and disappear into the murky lake waters.

Lucy quickly ran through the notes to refresh her memory showing how Felipe managed this, and she never got her hands dirty.

Azariah Weber, a client of Club Twilight, outright asked for a sit down with Lucy. He told Lucy he heard she sometimes helped with revenge when the law failed to rectify a crime committed.

Azariah's son at the time, sixteen years old, was bullied and beaten. He believed that because his son was gay, he was left for dead in an alley, but he survived after three months of physical therapy.

Once again, Lucy stepped in at Azariah's request for justice after months of no charges brought against the three attackers. The son pointed at the three teenagers outside a drug store to men appointed by Felipe at Lucy's request. The teens were scooped up into a van with hoods over their heads and taken away. Hours later, they were found roadside badly beaten, and not one of them could identify who attacked. Left with a warning, if they continued to bully people at school, they would never walk again on their own.

Darby knocked on the door and walked in to find Lucy curled up reading. "You know you're running out of time."

"I'm working on it," Lucy said. "I have one chance, and I must get it right."

Thirty minutes later, Lucy came down the spiral staircase dressed in her tight black leather pants, silk blouse, and vest.

"Ready for battle, Cat Woman," Darby said with a slight snicker.

"This is no laughing matter, and today is how I live the rest of my life or die," Lucy said, raising the black book. "These guys better come through."

She headed for the kitchen, then sat on a barstool and stared at her cell phone on the counter. From the black book, she dialed Ben Anderson's number first.

"Ben," Lucy said when he answered. "Sorry to call so early."

"No problem, I had a late-night case," he said. "Who is this?"

"Lucy Jones."

"Ms. Jones? I haven't heard from you since—"

Lucy cut him off. "No need to go there."

Ben agreed to meet her in one hour at a Café near his

condo on Magazine Street without question. She called Azariah Weber, and he met her in an hour and a half at the same café. The meeting was set as far apart as possible, and there simply wasn't enough time to further spread them.

Her next call was to Felipe. He was still on board and had his people ready, and his main worry was Lucy transferring his cash assets to his offshore account. She assured him six million dollars--the first of many--would go to his Panama account within the hour. Felipe had doubt in his voice when asking, indicating he was getting nervous. Like maybe he'd ship out of the United States and never could come back, and Lucy would run with his money.

Darby pulled the SUV around to the circle driveway, and they drove to the Burdette House before heading to the café. On the way Lucy called her banker in Panama and with her approval and a five number code the money was on its way to a new account she set up a day earlier for Felipe. He could draw money on the account from anywhere in the world. Then she texted Felipe the bank phone number and code to his account.

On arrival, Wanda walked with Lucy and found Beth attending homeschooling with a few other children who came to the house for refuge with their mothers.

"How is she adjusting?" Lucy asked.

"Surprisingly, good," Wanda said. "Not once asked about her father."

"Why would she? He was her father only by name." Lucy then pulled Wanda to the side. "You have the combination to my safe?"

"Yes. Why?"

"Just checking. Remember anything ever happens to me, go see my attorney, Barry Goldstein. He has power of attorney over all my business dealing, and you inherit everything should I disappear."

"Lucy?" Wanda asked. "What's going on?"

"Just a precaution," Lucy said, trying to work up a smile.

"Precaution!" Wanda whispered. "A precaution is taking an umbrella when it looks like rain."

Following Lucy through the house and out to the car, she asked again, "Lucy, what is going on?"

She did not reply. The door closed, and the SUV pulled away.

CHAPTER 32

THE MORNING COFFEE CROWD was long gone, and Lucy spotted Ben Anderson at a table, recognizable despite him gaining weight and growing a beard. Darby waited at the counter.

"Good morning, Ben," Lucy said.

He stood and shook her hand, and they exchanged a warm welcome. Lucy got right to the point when they took their seat. Ben listened while Lucy laid out how she needed his assistance. He didn't speak a word and shifted his eyes a few times. She felt he might have been looking to see if anyone were within an ear's length of hearing her. Lucy was very cautious and piped down even lower for his comfort. She went from start to finish without Ben asking a question.

Before he spoke, there was a long pause. "Knowing that asshole got what was coming to him after the legal system failed, yet justice was still served for my mother's death…"

"I hear a 'but' coming…" Lucy said.

"Lucy, I appreciate everything you've done."

"You came to me for justice, and I made it happen,"

Lucy lingered, her eyes shifted in thought, then stared him down. "Your shiny detective record is unblemished. Now it's time to pay your debt."

"What you're asking is borderline illegal."

"You're right, Ben, borderline, and I stuck my neck out to help you. I recommended Felipe Cruz, and between you two—it was handled. It was you that wanted satisfaction in your mother's death."

"Yes, but I never said kill the guy."

"That was the end result, and it was you that gave the order."

Ben's eyes became wide-eyed, and his expression was a blank stare. "Why are you doing this, after all this time."

"Debts don't expire, Ben. It's time for you to step up."

The last thing Lucy wanted to do was go to plan B, but she was prepared if necessary. She moistened her lips with a slight lick of her tongue. "Are you going to help?"

There were a lot of head shifting and body movements, then Ben took a paper napkin and

blotted sweat coming from his forehead.

"I'm sorry, Lucy, I can't."

"That's too bad. I counted on you," Lucy said and swung her eyes at Darby.

It was her clue to step behind Ben. Plan B was about to go into action.

Ben stood and extended his hand across the table. "No hard feelings."

"No, none at all," Lucy said. "Sit down!"

Darby grabbed him from the shoulders and forced him into the chair.

"Are you crazy, woman? Who are you?"

"My name is Darby, and I'm Lucy's bodyguard, trained in Martial Arts—don't make me
hurt you."

Ben pulled his coat back, showing his gun, and flipped out his badge. "I'm a cop. Touch me again, and I'll arrest you or shoot you right here."

"You'll be incapacitated before you can do either," Darby said with a look she could back up her statement.

Lucy pulled a recorder from her vest pocket and rewound the tape to the words spoken.

It was you that wanted satisfaction in your mother death. Yes, but I never said kill the guy.

"Don't make me go to the DA. There is a lot more on this tape from the conversation we had the day of your mother's attacker driving down the boat launch."

Lucy pulled a piece of paper from her purse and slipped it across the table to Ben. "Make sure you're at this corner tonight. When it goes down, you'll call your dispatch and say you'll take the call. The rest of the directions explain what I need."

Anger oozed from Ben, uncontrollable, and yet he sat motionlessly. He took the paper and jammed it into his pocket. Kicking the chair to the floor, he stormed out of the café.

"Is he going to do it?" Darby asked.

Lucy stared at the front entrance for the longest, then slowly focused on Darby. "If he doesn't, I am dead."

By the time Dr. Azariah Weber arrived, Lucy had two cups of coffee. Her anxiety calmed enough not to speak foolishly. They hugged it out, and he took a seat. Darby returned to her post, hoping she was not needed to convince Azariah.

"How can I help you, Lucy." Azariah wasted no time and seemed more sincere than Ben in returning a favor.

Lucy spelled it out quickly, missing no points. His reaction was slow in coming as he absorbed the details. When he took too long to answer, Lucy went on defense.

"How is your son?" Lucy asked. It was a way of reminding Azariah of her involvement in getting justice for his family.

"He's fine, Lucy. Times have changed, and he and his partner purchased a house and adopted a baby. Thanks for asking."

It was music to her ears that the teenager grew to be an admirable family man. She wasted no time and went into detail about what was needed. Even when he interrupted once for clarification, it didn't derail Lucy's thought process, and she got to the point.

Azariah's pause was the same as Ben's, and it didn't sit well with her. Her anxiety was moving up to a point she felt her face heat up and was sure it was bright red.

"There are ways I can make this happen," he said.

Lucy's heart felt like it was coming through her chest. That easy, Azariah agreed to a decision that could change the course of his career.

"Thank you," is all Lucy could muster up.

"Happy to help. When is this going down?"

"Tonight, close to midnight. Azariah, I will owe you," Lucy said.

"We're good. I knew one day you'd come calling," he smiled. "And Lucy, this is not as big a deal as you think."

"Really?"

"Bodies get mistakenly tagged and go missing for months, and some have no next to kin and never get claimed. I'll make it happen."

Azariah assured Lucy he'd be ready once again when the body showed up at the morgue. Lucy stared him down with Darby at her side until he got in his car.

"Is he bullshitting you just to get away from a face-to-face?" Darby asked.

"I hope not," Lucy said as she gave Azariah a wave when his car pulled from the curb.

Turning to Darby, she grabbed her shoulders. "Look at me. Anything goes south tonight, and I catch a bullet to my head. You make sure you kill Ben before morning because it will be his screw up that killed me. Then take the money I left for you and run."

"Under my bed?"

"Yes, I left a million dollars in cash."

Darby's eyes spun around like cherries on a slot machine. "Well, boss, for that much money—if you don't go down tonight by Bozzano, I may have to take you out myself."

They broke into a well-needed laugh.

"If you live through the night, do I get to keep the money?"

Lucy gave a grin.

Darby answered her own question, "I suppose not."

CHAPTER 33

THE REST OF THAT day was spent on the phone, ensuring everything was in place for that night. Lucy checked with Felipe, and he was not only ready but sounded excited to start a new life. A little nervous that one misstep and he'd be dead, but he would take that chance on a new life. His money was in place, and he sounded excited to move on without looking over his shoulder.

A private jet set to depart from the New Orleans East airport could go unnoticed late at night at an airport without commercial flights.

It was time to make the call, and she pressed Tony Bozzano's number. It rang twice, then Big Sally picked up. A brief conversation, she got her message across that she would be at the Red Onion Restaurant with Felipe at ten that night. There was one catch she wanted Mr. Bozzano to have a sit-down with Felipe.

The words still ring in Lucy's ear when Sally shouted. *Are you crazy? Bozzano have a sit down in a public restaurant with a drug dealer?*

Lucy planned hard for his reaction, and she had to follow through. "I think you should hear Felipe out."

"What the hell Lucy? You were to direct us to his location, not broker a deal."

"Financially, it's good for everyone."

"Bozzano is not looking to make a deal with a man that tried to kill him. He just wants the bastard dead."

Lucy pulled all stops and demanded Bozzano meet with Felipe. If the meeting did not go well, he could walk Felipe out front to his death.

Then Lucy pulled a Bozzano trick and spoke. "Be at the Red Onion Restaurant, 9:00 P.M," and hung up.

When she got off the phone, her hand shook, then her body, and she rushed to the bathroom. Darby came running when she heard Lucy release her lunch and everything else in her stomach down the toilet.

"You, okay?" Darby said at the door.

"Yeah, give me a minute," she replied.

It was thirty minutes before Lucy surfaced. "Let's go. We must follow through like this is going to happen."

At the end of Royal Street, the retail shops turned into residential shotgun houses in the French Quarter. Some lived in the rear of their one-room makeshift store with items for sale hanging on the front porch.

Darby dropped Lucy in front of a business called *The House of Cards,* with a slogan underneath that read: *Believe nothing you see.* Cosmo, the only name Lucy knew for the owner, met her at the front entrance.

Cosmo was a magician with a shady background and a chemistry degree which he never used for good. He kept a low profile, and a connection to him was usually a recommendation from a trusted person who had done business with him before. His specialty was handguns with no serial numbers, fake identification, driver's licenses, passports, and even college diplomas from the best of schools.

Cosmo met Lucy at the front steps leading to the open porch. He was dressed in his usual weird clothing—a white shirt, a black coat with tails, and a top hat. He once told Lucy that the outfit was like a uniform to him and worn every day.

"My lady," he said, reaching for her hand. "How nice to see you."

"Are you ready?" Lucy whispered.

He didn't answer and walked her in. "I'll be with you in a second, Ms. Lucy."

Then he finished with a customer putting her purchase in a bag. "Thank you, and let me know how your son likes the magic set."

Once the woman was down the steps, he quickly locked the door and flipped a closed sign facing out.

"Follow me," he said to Lucy.

Walking through a dark hallway to the back of the house, she would have been afraid had she not known Cosmo was just a weird guy. She hadn't ruled out a serial killer, so she kept her hand on a gun in her purse.

He pulled a black leather vest off a hanger. "He wears this over a shirt for the best illusion. When he is ready, pull this cord, and a pocket inside will allow him to breathe without showing his chest moving."

"Any room for error?" Lucy asked, looking at the garment that appeared to be any vest off the rack at a department store.

"None," Cosmo replied. "You get one pull."

"What if it fails?"

"My lady, I'm the best. It will not fail."

"Will it hurt?"

He chuckled. "It will hurt like hell and maybe inflict a burn mark here or there. Don't worry—you're not the one wearing the vest."

A bag covered the garment, and Lucy waltzed out the house like any customer. Darby pulled up, and she jumped into the backseat of the SUV.

Darby carried the hanger in and unveiled it to Felipe, at his home. She explained what happened when the cord was pulled.

"You get one shot," Darby said.

"No dress rehearsal?" Felipe said, turning to Lucy.

"Nope, don't pull the cord until you're ready."

Felipe tried the vest on, and it fit snug, just like Cosmo said it should. He appeared less confident than earlier that morning.

"It's going to be okay. Think about tonight when you're sitting on a private plane jetting across the Gulf of Mexico to your new home, free of this life."

When Lucy's phone vibrated in her purse, she quickly looked at the screen, not wanting to miss a call from Big Sally. The last person she wanted to talk to at this time was Stella, and that's the name that flashed on the screen. She was torn between answering or letting it go to voice mail. The first thing that ran through her mind was the police found out Wiggins had a daughter. It was also close to her shift ending, and she may have wanted a flirty conversation with a glass of wine at the Carousel Bar. The romance wasn't on her agenda today, but she could use a cocktail.

Lucy stepped away from Felipe and answered. "Well, what a pleasant surprise."

"Not so," Stella said. "Just a heads up." Then her voice went to a whisper. "There is a tail on Felipe Cruz, so stay away from him."

Lucy glanced at Felipe, and he was too engrossed with Darby fitting the shoulders of the vest to be bothered with her.

"What's going down?"

"Lucy, it's way out of my hands," Stella said, then paused. "I heard the ATF is waiting for a judge to sign off on an indictment tonight. Once approved, the ATF will come down on him with force."

"Why?" She asked anyway knowing they could pick up Felipe on several charges on any day.

"They got a tip. Felipe got to Wiggins's house first and moved guns—most of the weapons. I think they will tie him to gun smuggling…anything to get him back in jail."

"When?"

"ATF likes to take their marks down in the middle of the night," she said, then her voice went even lower. "Lucy, stay away from him."

"Stella, I have no connection with Felipe, and I haven't seen him in weeks," Lucy said loud, purposely for him to hear. It got a reaction, and Felipe stepped closer.

"Well, thanks for the heads up," Lucy said, her eyes shifting with fear. "But as I said, I haven't seen him."

"Lucy, one more thing. Child services interviewed Wigging's neighbors, and he had a daughter, and the neighbor has not seen the child since the father was killed."

"Really?"

"They think Felipe may have killed the father and kidnapped the child," Stella paused. "From that point, who knows what he may have done with her."

"That's not Felipe's style," Lucy said, keeping calm.

"I know you have your ear to the ground. Anything comes up on the girl—you let me know."

"I sure will, Stella," Lucy said and hung up.

Felipe and Darby stood like a deer in headlights.

"ATF is following you and will take you down sometime after midnight," Lucy said, walking to the door. "And they know about Beth. Let's go, Darby." She then turned back to Filipe. "Felipe, you're one lucky man."

"How's that?"

"You have a plan already in the works to live happily ever after—if we pull it off."

"There are no ifs!" Felipe shouted to Lucy as she got to the car. "I'm not going back to jail. This must work."

Darby drove Lucy home, and she got out and leaned into Darby's window. "Find Big Sally, where he is Bozzano will be. They must be at the restaurant by nine tonight, and any indication they are not heading there… You must persuade them."

"How am I supposed to do that?"

"I don't know, Darby," Lucy said. It was the first time Lucy showed fear. "It's our only way out of this mess."

CHAPTER 34

It was time to prepare for the carefully planned meeting, but Lucy still wasn't sure all the players would show up. She got dressed with a second Old Fashioned under her belt. It wasn't as good as Darby made, but it served its purpose. Her glass raised to the mirror. *It's been a great ride.* Then she took the last gulp of the cocktail.

A car horn blew at the front entrance, and Lucy came down. Wanda drove from the Garden District to pick her up. Unusual, but when hearing Darby was on a mission, she stepped up to drive and not have Lucy take a taxi. It also gave Wanda a chance for a one-on-one with her daughter, which seemed to happen less these days.

"You okay?" Wanda asked as soon as they drove off. "Can you share anything with me?"

"Mom, it's best you don't know the details," Lucy said, cutting her off.

To ensure the subject was dropped, Lucy made a call to Darby. "Tell me I'm not driving to the restaurant to eat alone?"

"I don't know," Darby said. "I'm down the street

from Bozzano's house, and Sally is still in the vehicle waiting."

"That's a good sign," Lucy said, perking up. "Maybe he's changing clothes. If he was done for the night, the SUV would have moved from the front of the house, and his goons would stand post out front till morning."

"Wait! Sally just got out of the car."

"Do you see Bozzano?"

Darby looked the best she could in the dark. Then pulled night goggles from the console. "Yes, Bozzano is walking out with a coat in hand, and he got in the car."

"Darby, if he doesn't head to the Red Onion—you know what to do."

"I will not let you down," Darby said and ended the call.

Wanda pulled up to the Red Onion Restaurant. "I always wanted to try this place, heard it was good."

"Mom, stop with the small talk," Lucy said, then leaned over and gave her a kiss on the cheek. "I love you."

"Lucy, isn't there someone that can help? Your cop friend Stella or your underground associates?" Wanda asked, holding tears back. "What am I supposed to do!"

Lucy stepped out and bent down into the driver's window. "Go home, maybe say a little prayer and keep the TV on…there might be some breaking news later."

In the restaurant, Lucy tipped the hostess for the booth she requested. Sitting, she ordered a drink for some false courage before anyone showed up. Startled when her cell phone rang, she yanked it up, seeing Darby's name on the screen.

"Give it to me."

"They made a stop and picked up three," Darby said. "Bozzano is coming with muscle."

"Nothing we didn't expect," Lucy said. "Is he headed this way?"

"Hold, I'll know in a second. Not good," Darby said. "They turned away from downtown."

"Darby! You must stop them!" Lucy said in a low voice and still got the message across.

"Boss, there are four thugs in the car, plus I know Bozzano is packing."

"Do whatever it takes."

"Dammit, not now!" Darby shouted. "A cop pulled me over."

"Were you speeding?"

"No, I was tailing him from far behind."

"Maybe Big Sally spotted you, and Bozzano called one of his cops on his payroll. Keep the phone open."

Lucy couldn't make out the conversation and waited on Darby to return. The waiter brought her a cocktail, and she sipped quickly to calm her anxiety.

"Lucy?"

"Yeah," she said, putting the phone to her ear.

"You were right. The cop pulled me from the car and checked my license. When I asked why he pulled me over, he slammed the butt of his gun into the rear taillight, then said it's obvious you have a broken taillight."

"Take some side streets and get over here. Remember, I don't expect this to go well. You must be in place and ready to fire. Darby," Lucy paused. "You must be dead on target."

Lucy clicked the phone to off and dropped it in her

purse. Then she spotted Felipe walking in as planned. He was alone, and it was the only way this could work, and the part Felipe most resisted.

"It's show time," Felipe said when he took a seat.

"Hopefully, you do an Oscar performance tonight," Lucy said, offering a nervous smile. "Unlike the movies, there will be no retakes."

Lucy's cell rang. "Yes, Darby."

"Bozzano is out front of the restaurant, and the muscle is checking things out before they bring him in. It's happening. Be careful, Lucy."

Lucy barely got the phone in her purse when she spotted Big Sally at the front entrance. His eyes scanned the restaurant and stopped at two men at the bar, and it was apparent Bozzano had muscle inside too.

"Felipe just don't do anything stupid," Lucy said, tapping his leg.

"As long as the old man doesn't get out of line, it will go smooth," he replied.

"Just think of white sand and a cool breeze with a cocktail in your hand," Lucy tried to paint a picture.

"There are many obstacles before I smell the saltwater in the air."

Bozzano walked like the king had arrived, Big Sally in the lead and two men behind. Felipe knew the drill and stood shaking Bozzano's hand and allowing Sally to frisk him without patrons knowing it happened.

Sally grinned as his hand went over Felipe's back. "Do you really think a bulletproof vest will stop me from putting a bullet in your head?"

Felipe returned the same nasty grin.

"What about Lucy?" Sally asked Bozzano.

He did this wrinkle nose thing and said with a raspy voice. "Lucy, you're planning to kill me tonight?"

She calmly said with her best smile, then clutched her purse. "Mr. Bozzano, I plan to make your life easier and enrich you behind your wildest dreams, making your family rich for generations."

Lucy watched Felipe scan the room, apparently for Bozzano's bodyguards. Her eyes drifted to Big Sally, who stood within a few feet and didn't break his stone face appearance. She ordered a bottle of Cristal Champagne to break the intense mood. There wasn't a word spoken until the waiter brought the bubbly and poured three glasses.

With a tilted head, Bozzano watched the waiter walk away. She then turned to the table and stared silently.

Lucy picked her glass up for a toast, and she paused when no one else did.

"I want you to know I have never agreed to a sit down outside my own restaurant," Bozzano said. "You have thirty seconds for your pitch."

Lucy sipped her champagne with a side glance at Felipe. She saw his expression change—knowing he never liked being talked down to.

"Twenty-five seconds," Bozzano said.

"I never ordered you dead. Juan Vargas approached me, and I refused," Felipe talked fast and left it out there for the boss man to respond.

Bozzano rubbed his face. "Is that the best you have? Funny, Juan is the only person that can confirm your statement, but he's dead. I heard he drove himself into the lake," Tony laughed. "That's the way I heard the story—what the hell? Maybe he wasn't driving."

"Please, hear me out?" Lucy said and was quickly shut down.

"This is his meeting," Bozzano said, eyeballing Felipe.

Lucy quickly saw the mood of the conversation run from bad to worse and interrupted. "Listen to me, Tony! Who came to you about Juan wanting to take you down? It was me!"

"What was it you said?" Tony rubbed his face again. "A dream, yeah, you call it your night terrors. You think I'm going to believe a dream?"

"The two guys that set you up were hired by Juan," Felipe threw in quickly.

"They were your men!" Tony shouted and pounded the table, which got the attention of many people.

"No," Felipe whispered, leaning over the table. "They were freelance, and I've used them once," Felipe said, during his best to keep his composure. "Come on, Tony, we all use outside sources. This just happened to be men I used once before, and it doesn't mean I was involved."

Felipe was a gambling man, putting the conversation at thirty percent. That meant it was a seventy percent chance Bozzano wasn't buying his bullshit.

"To show good faith, I'll give you a hundred thousand for—" Felipe said. A long silence with eyes shifting went on. "Call it a misunderstanding."

Bozzano did that thing with his nose again. "Misunderstanding? Automatic weapons in the linen closet, enough to take down everyone in the restaurant?"

Lucy jumped in. "And ten percent of the drug money, and I'll wash it to you free." She waited for a response and got another ugly sweep of his hand across his face. "My company will rent the retail space you have on Canal Street and pay a million a year, and that's a million dollars a year clean money." Lucy drove it home hard without a blink. "Felipe dies, and your money train stops."

You could cut the tension at the table with a knife. Felipe slipped his hand into a side pocket of Lucy's purse. A gun was right where she said it would be if he was hauled off by Bozzano's goons. He tucked the gun into the back of the vest and into his belt.

Tony shot a side glance at Sally, and he jumped like a dog on command and stood at the table side for his orders.

"We're leaving," Bozzano said, standing. "Felipe, don't make a scene, or I'll kill you here in this nice restaurant."

"Please, Tony? What do you want?" Lucy had no choice but to beg.

There was a long pause then the boss man spoke with a sharp tongue, "I want Felipe dead." Then he shot Big Sally a nod. They walked to the exit. Bozzano, in step with Sally and Felipe, were followed by two thugs. Lucy ran to keep up with the pace and maybe get one last plea in.

They hit the open air, and Felipe scanned to locate Darby. But she wasn't visible, and he could only hope she was in position. Lucy's plan was perfect if it worked, and the gun would be used if he was forced into the back seat of a car. Bozzano insulted him one too many times throughout the meeting, and he toyed with a slight change to the plan.

Felipe slipped his hand under the vest, and with one quick move, he pulled the gun and fired one shot at Bozzano. Hitting him in the head, he dropped like a sack of potatoes.

People scattered, and their screams echoed off the buildings. There was mass confusion as people took cover.

Bozzano bled out at Big Sally's feet as Sally pulled his gun. Before his hand was extended, a bullet hit him in the shoulder, and the gun dropped to the ground.

Every second counted, and Lucy screamed at Felipe, "Do it!"

The second bodyguard came from hiding, his gun pointed, and that is when Felipe pulled the cord on the vest. Six shots exploded in his vest, and he stumbled and dropped to the ground.

Bozzano was attended to, but it was easy to see he was dead with the right side of his head missing. Sally attended to his own wound, and another bodyguard stepped up. He lifted his hand, aimed at Felipe's body, and shouted. "You bastard!" Then another bullet fired in the darkness, hitting the man perfectly in his forearm. He dropped to the ground, and the gun slid away from him.

Sirens were heard far away, and Darby went into action. She disassembled a high-power rifle, packed it in a gun case, and moved the SUV to the center of the street. Only Lucy stood. The injured and the dead body were on the ground. All others ran and took shelter. Lucy flipped the gun used to kill Bozzano into the car's passenger seat and Darby pulled away.

CHAPTER 35

Before the police or rescue, vehicles arrived on the scene. Ben Anderson pulled up, went to his trunk, pulled a white sheet, and placed it over Felipe.

Lucy was placed in the back seat of Ben's black Dodge Charger. She looked at Ben and whispered a simple, "Thank you."

"Don't thank me, don't talk to me, just forget my name," he said. "I'll handle my end." Seconds later, police swarmed the area, and paramedics rushed to the wounded.

Ben raised his badge over his head, announcing his name and rank, indicating he was the lead in this investigation.

"Got another dead one here," Ben shouted, pointing to Bazzano. An officer brought another white sheet, and the body was covered.

Forensics arrived and took pictures of the scene. Paramedics patched the wounded the best they could. The injured waited to give their statements before going to the hospital.

A waiter walked the outline of the crime scene tape and offered bottled water to the police and people involved in the shooting. Lucy accepted as her mind wandered, and her hand shook as the bottle reached her lips.

She made it to this point without getting herself killed, but most of all, Ben came through. The plan was for Felipe to appear dead and disappear in the night, never to be seen, and Bozzano would never look for him. It would have been classified as a gang shooting taking out a lead cartel member. The gun was brought in only as a defense if the vest didn't work. Felipe wanted a backup plan, and Lucy had no clue his goal was to kill the boss man.

More parts to the puzzle had to work before it was a successful mission. Still, thinking of living in a world without Bozzano and Felipe brought butterflies to her stomach.

The second in command took Lucy's statement from the car's back seat at Ben's request. She explained they had dinner, and when they walked out, a bullet was fired. She thought Bozzano was hit first, then several more shots were fired, and Felipe fell to the ground and wasn't sure who was hit since she had taken cover. Lucy paused when seeing the black Coroner's Office van stopped in the street. Dr. Azariah Weber, the driver, got out and walked directly to Ben Anderson. Her heart raced as all the players came through for the most extensive criminal scam.

The formality of an investigation was to get statements and mark off the best they could the distance the shots were fired. No information was the same. Big Sally said Felipe pulled a gun and fired a shot at Bozzano. One bodyguard said he heard the blast, but his back was turned. The detective looked for a handgun Sally described, but none was found.

Dr. Weber pulled the sheet from the side of Felipe. "Four direct hits in his chest," he said,

staring up at Ben. Then put his fingers against Felipe's neck and talked into a recorder. "No pulse, time of death 10:22 P.M, from four shots to the chest." He stopped the recorder.

Weber called for a stretcher and got a little resistance from the forensics investigator when he moved the body. Ben stepped in and took charge, saying he wanted the street cleaned of dead bodies.

Dr. Weber referred to a memo the mayor sent around on murder cases. The priority was to get dead bodies from the view of tourists and residents. Details of the murder would be determined at the morgue. The forensics team backed away, and once the area was cleared, the doctor pulled the sheet back over Felipe.

"You okay?"

A faint "yes," was whispered by Felipe. "It hurts like a bitch."

Dr. Weber moved his upper body of Felipe with help from another with his legs. The stretcher was moved to the van's rear, then loaded into the truck, and Dr. Weber drove off.

Lucy cut her interview short, saying she was too upset to continue once seeing the Coroner's office leave with Felipe and Darby pulling up. She assured the officer she would be downtown first thing in the morning to go over her statement. A nod from Ben gave the okay, and she stepped from the back seat of the police vehicle into her SUV.

Darby turned the corner and shouted, "You did it!"

"Oh my god," Lucy said. They went on like teenagers coming home from a date.

They settled down, and Lucy pointed out, it was far from over. There were a few more things that needed to happen without a hitch.

She made a phone call, she waited for more rings than she felt comfortable with, and finally, someone answered.

"Tower. Andrew speaking."

"Hi, Andrew," Lucy said without giving her name.

"I'll call you back," he said and hung up.

Within seconds he called Lucy. "Sorry I didn't want to talk on that line," he said.

"Are you ready?"

"That's what took so long to answer. The wheels are down on approach."

"Great! Now, Andrew, the aircraft is off the logbooks."

"Lucy, this is a regional airport. The next flight is FedEx at 3:00 A.M., and next out is the news team at 6:00 A.M., so you have a window of close to three hours. There will be no record of this plane ever stopping.

"Andrew, thank you. The Burdette House will send a check to your children's school to prepay next year's tuition, and no money passes through your hands."

"It works for me," Andrew said and hung up.

CHAPTER 36

WITHIN MINUTES OF THE coroner's office van driving off, a voice shouted out.

"Can I take this damn sheet off my face?"

"My passengers don't usually talk to me on the way to the morgue," Dr. Weber replied.

Felipe sat up and asked his name.

"Dr. Azariah Weber, New Orleans Coroner's office."

"Why are you doing this for me?"

"Has nothing to do with you—I did it for Lucinda Jones."

"Risk your career and maybe go to jail. You must have been very indebted to Lucy," Felipe said, digging for more information.

"She helped me out once," he said. "I believe in paying back."

A block from the morgue, the doctor stopped the van and stepped back to the stretcher. In his hand, he held a syringe.

"I'm covering you up now. There will be someone to help to move you inside. If you move, breathe, blink an eye, or do anything to give away that you're not dead—I will inject you."

"And what does that do?" Felipe asked.

"You're dead—for real in five seconds."

The doctor said he would go directly into the freezer for five minutes. Enough time for him to clear everyone out of the basement morgue.

"What!" Felipe shouted. "No one said anything about me going into a freezer."

"It must have been a part Lucy left out. You don't have a choice. Agree, or I'll stick you now, and you'll never know how long you were in the freezer."

There was little Felipe could say. They were at the point of no return. He went back under the sheet and did his best to dream of the island, white sand like he had never seen, a blue ocean, and a cold beer in his hand.

In the garage of the morgue, he heard a man's voice when the rear doors were opened.

"What you have, doc?"

"Not sure, maybe some gang banger who got taken out."

"Doc? Can we put him on ice till morning?" the young man made a face. "I had a ten-hour day."

"No problem, I'll handle everything."

The gurney was taken from the van and pushed next to a stainless-steel moveable on a table.

"Put him in number twenty-two."

The assistant rolled the stainless-steel device to the freezer. Under the sheet, Felipe did everything to stay calm. He thought of the islands again, the warm weather, but nothing prepared him for the cold darkness and the sound of the freezer door closing.

It seemed like an hour for Felipe in the freezer, but only four minutes had passed before Dr. Weber got the assistant out and locked the doors.

Door twenty-two opened, and Felipe rolled out on the gurney. His lips pale, and he shook, but the doctor went to work.

The vest was opened, and makeup was used to show a bullet entry at each hole. It took little since the explosives used to simulate the gunshot burnt Felipe's chest at the impact.

"Hold your breath," he said and took several pictures from different angles.

When he finished, Felipe couldn't get up quick enough. The doctor poured Felipe a cup of coffee from the leftover pot, still hot.

Dr. Weber's cell phone rang, and he looked at the screen. "Your ride is here."

"Good," Felipe said. Then took a sip of hot coffee, ran to a sink, and spit it out. "What the hell kind of coffee is this?"

"Sometimes the coffee sucks up the dead body smell. I got used to it."

Felipe rinsed his mouth with water. Then put on green scrubs. He helped move a body not claimed in six months to freezer number twenty-two. Felipe's clothes were placed in the freezer with the body.

"How do you explain no bullet holes?"

The doctor gave a grin. "My report goes to the DA's office, pictures, and all. Once he signs off, I will show a signed statement from your wife to have the body cremated. No one from the DA's office wants to see the real body."

Mostly, the morgue was closed for the night. Except for Dr. Weber, who was on call, no one else was around. It took less than two minutes for Lucy to back up to the dock and Felipe to jump in the back of the SUV.

"Make sure these papers are signed, and a copy of the wife's driver's license is returned tomorrow."

"Azariah," Lucy said through the rear window. "I couldn't have done this without you."

"I know, and Lucy, don't ever come calling again."

From the back, Felipe popped up, "Mama, we did it!"

Lucy pulled the same handgun used to kill Bozzano and pointed it at his head. "Why did you off Bozzano? It was not in the plan."

"I know, but the more I thought about it—Bozzano might come after my wife and kids. Even knowing I am dead."

"No! He would not. In time it would have blown over."

"I'm not so sure. My way, he is never coming after anyone."

Lucy cocked the pistol, "I should kill you right here. With the same gun you used on Bozzano. I'll change my story: I saw you kill Bozzano, and someone turned the same gun on you before you were riddled yourself with fake bullets. Which I also didn't know anything about."

"Lucy don't go crazy on me now," Felipe's said. His eyes widened when he saw the fear on Darby's face through the mirror.

"Lucy?" Darby said. "We're close to the airport, and this will all be over." There was no reply. "Or I can continue to the bayou and kill him there—but not in the car."

A long pause had Felipe sweating.

"Airport," Lucy said and pointed the gun down.

The SUV rolled into the tarmac to a jet ready to fly. Felipe boarded, and he no sooner got on board than the stairs went up and the plane taxied. They stood outside and waited for the plane to get airborne.

Darby took the gun off the seat and broke it into three parts. One piece went in the storm drain inside the airport, and she planned the other pieces for successive stops on the way home.

"Here she comes," Lucy said, hearing the jet engines roar down the runway. Lucy turned and hugged Darby. "It's over. It's really over!"

CHAPTER 37

THE FOLLOWING MORNING LUCY walked through her lakefront home with a sigh of relief. Lucy was never incarcerated other than some overnight jail stays as a teenager. But her body tingled as if she had been released from a twenty-year prison term.

"What do I need to do today," Darby asked. "Any loose ends to wrap up?"

Lucy reached for two boxes of Aunt Sally's Pralines from the bottom of the liquor cabinet.

"So now you hide the sweets from me?" Darby said with her lip out.

"Open it," Lucy said.

Darby pulled the lid off, "eight creamy pralines,"

"Keep digging in the decorative grass."

"Wow, who's the lucky recipient?" Darby separated the grass. "Four packs?"

"Twenty thousand in each box," Lucy said. "Felipe's gift to Ben Anderson and Dr. Azariah Weber for their help."

"I'll deliver it personally, in their hands."

The doorbell rang, and Darby peeked at the monitor in the kitchen. "Right on time, Rosa Cruz."

"You look pretty good for a recent widow," Lucy said, greeting her.

They hugged it out. "Is it over? He's okay?"

"As far as I know," Lucy said.

"When can I go?" Rosa asked.

"Give it thirty days," Lucy replied. "I'll text him, and he'll send the plane."

Darby got her to sign the coroner's office papers, and Rosa left smiling.

They no sooner got back to the kitchen than Lucy's cell phone rang. She looked at the screen and was surprised it took this long for Stella to call. "Here," she passed the phone to Darby. "Tell her I'm in the shower."

Lucy got dressed and left Darby talking with Stella, telling her side of the almost-death experience. She poured it on thick, telling Stella she was parked down the street waiting for Lucy when gunshots were heard. Darby explained Lucy was shaken but okay and would probably have many sleepless nights over the brutal slaughter.

Lucy came down as Darby hung up, "Thanks. That was a half hour of my life I'll never get back."

"Better you than me, "Lucy said with a smile. "Let's go."

As they drove, Darby talked about one part of Stella's conversation. "Are you aware Stella had a task force bust one of his stash houses?"

"What do you mean?"

"She got a tip late last night where Felipe stored the guns. It was in some ship container. They got the guns, uncut coke, and four of Felipe's top men."

"My god, that slick bastard. He had a fifty-fifty chance

of getting killed or off for a new life. Either way, he didn't want anyone in his crew to take over. Felipe turned the cops onto his own people, and his drug empire has crumbled."

"Lucy, the day just keeps getting better," Darby gave her a smile in the mirror.

The SUV pulled up at Tulane and Broad Street in front of police headquarters. The Detective's Division was on the first floor, and her heels tapping on the marble floor echoed through the building. A door with frosted glass in the center read Detective Ben Anderson in black letters.

Greeted quickly, Lucy was taken to a room and met Ben and one women police detective.

"Thank you for coming, Ms. Jones, "Ben said. "I know how hard this must be for you."

Lucy did her best not to grin at his formal greeting, but he kept with the program. His career was on the line if anything failed so he could be nothing but pleasant.

"Please sit," he said, pulling a chair out for Lucy.

Darby walked down the ramp that led to underground parking for the police with Aunt Sally's box of pralines. She found parking with a plaque on the wall labeled *Detective Ben Anderson*. The black Dodge Charger was backed into the space. Darby was not surprised the doors were open. Who would consider stealing something with so many cops around? She opened the passenger door and placed the box of pralines on the seat.

Darby still had time to walk to the coroner's office and spoke with the receptionist in the lobby.

"May I help you?" An older woman who looked like she came with the place asked.

Darby placed the box on the counter. "Dr. Azariah Weber, please."

"He's busy at this time," she said. "I'll be happy to give this to him."

"I'm sorry, but I'm with a delivery service, and the requirement is for me to put this in Dr. Azariah Weber's hands."

It took a little pursuing, but the lady called for Dr. Weber, who refused to come until Darby said it was a delivery from Lucinda Jones. She was sure the last thing the doctor wanted was any connection going on around the office between him and Lucy.

"Can I help you," Dr. Weber said when he got there.

"Ms. Jones wanted to thank you for how her cousin Felipe Cruz was handled," Darby smiled and handed him the box. "Just a little something for your sweet tooth."

The doctor, who had seen dead people under the worse conditions and then took them back to his table and cut on them like a butcher carving out filets, looked white and nervous.

"Oh, and she asked that I give this to you, too," Darby said and handed over a sealed envelope.

The doctor opened and glanced at the letter inside and quickly put it in his jacket. "Well, please thank her and let her know the DA released Felipe's body, and his wife has directed us to have him cremated."

"I'll be sure to deliver the message."

Darby got a text that Lucy was ready, and she walked the block and met her at the car.

"Great news," Darby said.

"Can it get any better?" Lucy said with a wide smile.

"Felipe's clothes are going up in flames in about an hour," Darby said. "It's a first. His garments turned into ashes will have a death certificate under the name of Felipe Cruz."

CHAPTER 38

One month later.

LIFE WAS GOOD FOR Councilwoman Lucinda Jones. She worked on city projects neglected and attended meetings regularly.

The *Times-Picayune* newspaper that once featured *Mob Boss and Drug Cartel gunned down in the streets of New Orleans* slowly disappeared to follow-up stores buried in the back of the newspaper. Media always featured the most recent big story until it was replaced with another tragedy.

A story like a mass shooting had a longer life in a newspaper than on television. Lucy had not heard a word mentioned on the local 10 P.M. news since the third day of the shooting.

The restaurant closed for a week, crews came in, workers washed the sidewalk with bleach and even slapped a new coat of paint on the front of the building, and the owner took a well-earned vacation. The restaurant re-opened and operated as if nothing had happened.

Felipe's street runners dried up selling drugs on the corner in the French Quarter. Some moved on to other cities or may have changed their lives for the better and got real jobs. Lucy didn't care, and the city was better off without Felipe and Bozzano.

Lucy never looked back or questioned her decision. It was a chance to get out from under Felipe's thumb, but she never dreamed he would take out Bozzano on the same night.

Two nights before this day, Rosa Cruz and her son boarded a private jet during the night, and it would make two stops as a decoy before meeting up with Felipe. Rosa carried a suitcase of cash that Lucy had packed after she took her fee and a bonus for carrying out the scam.

Neither Lucy nor Felipe would ever hurt for money. The apartments, strip shopping centers, and retail stores that laundered their drug money were now profitable without the dirty money.

Lucy even smoothed things out with Stella, and they could now be in the same room without wanting to kill each other. This was partly because Detective Stella James got a bump to Sergeant Major from the takedown of arms dealer Oscar Sanchez, who was heading to federal prison for the next fifteen years.

The one issue that weighed on Lucy was Beth Wiggins. She still lived at Burdette House and went to the same school, driven by one lady on time every morning. Beth's grades improved assisted by a high-school teacher living in protection from a husband who beat her and left her for dead. He was still on the run and promised he'd find her.

The day finally came, and it was not by luck that the child services case for Beth Wiggins would be decided by Judge Elton Bordelon. Lucy took over all of Felipe's political connections. She thought was it was a shame to let a good judge on the take go unused. Felipe had trained them well.

That morning Lucy walked into court with her lawyer and Beth at her side. Gail Trahan with Child Services recommended Beth go to a foster home, and she would be with other children, parents, a male and female that had raised their own children.

Lucy's lawyer took the floor.

"Your honor, Beth Wiggins's grades have improved with a full-time tutor. She is exposed to other children that live at Burdette House, and she has a bedroom with three girls her age. Beth has two mothers who look after her needs and qualify to help with homework," he paused and picked up some papers from the table.

The judge looked over his glasses at Gail Trahan, and his head shook from side to side.

The lawyer continued, "And finally, your honor. Ms. Jones will see that Beth Wiggins is under doctor's care to ensure her mental health. In addition, Ms. Jones has placed money in a trust for Beth and two other children living at Burdette House to go to Louisiana State when they graduate from high school."

The lawyer walked the floor silently, his head down. "Your honor, Beth Wiggins has never had a normal childhood. She traveled with her thief of a father and didn't remember her mother. The only woman in her life was an occasional girlfriend of the father."

He stopped and stood at the podium and looked at the

judge. "Your honor please don't put this child through any more abuse. Let Beth Wiggins live with Lucy Jones in the Burdette House."

Judge Bordelon gave a sharp look down from his podium to Gail.

"Ms. Jones, please stand," the judge said. "Was all of this presented to Child Services before this hearing?"

"Yes, your honor, we did our best to work with Gail Trahan and her staff. Their answer was Beth was better off in the system."

"Thank you, Ms. Jones," he said and turned to Gail.

"Mrs. Trahan, please stand. I question why this is in my court. Your job is to see that unfortunate and neglected children are taken care of. What could be a better fit than this child living in a house well cared for by several women."

"Your honor, if I may," Gail said.

"You may not!" Judge Bordelon said and slammed his gavel down. "Beth Wiggins is put under the care of Lucinda Jones. Case dismissed."

CHAPTER 39

At 8:00 P.M. the same night, two valets stood outside Lucy's Lakefront mansion. Cars pulled to the curb, and the drivers stepped out, handed their keys, and walked away. Entering the house, a waiter stood with glasses of champagne, welcoming everyone.

Poolside, Lucy stood sipping champagne, looking glamorous, much like a movie star. The woman praised her form-fitting dress draped to the back, allowing her Jimmy Choo shoes to show in the front.

Waiters passed finger food, and there were two open bars.

"They are here," Darby said to Lucy's ear in a whisper.

Lucy greeted all the people from Burdette House as they stepped off a chartered bus. No one was left behind, including the children, and Beth escorted three teens upstairs to the media room for food, drinks, and movies.

The women of the Burdette House were much like college students on date night. They rooted through clothes Lucy had sent over from a department store and did each other's hair and makeup.

It was a special night for Lucy and her guests. She wanted

to give back to the community and the women who worked so hard without a thought of ever having an everyday life. She didn't wish to have the recognition. It was enough to have joy in her heart she came out of this ordeal alive.

"Ms. Lucy," Judge Bordelon said, touching her arm.

Lucy hoped he'd come since the invite read to join Councilwoman for a Gala Event. He showed up with his wife, who introduced herself and praised Lucy for stepping up for Beth.

It touched Lucy to hear the woman say she had been in foster care from twelve years old until she was allowed on her own.

The wife whispered, "I only wish I had someone like you to step up when I was pushed from family to family—who were only in it for the money the city allowed."

"Judge Bordelon," Lucy said. "Don't leave tonight without taking a box of Aunt Sally's Pralines home, and it's a special box just for you."

The judge gave a slight smile. "Lucy, no need for gifts. "Beth's case was close to my heart, as you have heard from my wife, and I am pleased it landed in my court."

"I understand, but don't leave without your pralines," Lucy insisted.

At the bar, Lucy asked for an Old Fashioned. Darby jumped in front of the bartender, "I'll make her drink. She's a tough customer."

Darby brought three cocktails to a poolside table for Lucy. "Why three drinks? Trying to get me hammered?"

"No," Darby said. "Lucy, you're like a cat with nine lives."

"I don't know what I did to deserve all this. Lord knows I have not been a good person."

"Lucy, you have done more for people in this district than anyone," Darby said, raising one glass. "Cheers! How you did it, where the money came from—is all behind you now."

Darby stood with her drink. "This is where I take off."

"Hello, Lucy," Stella said, sitting. "Thanks for inviting me." She reached over and held Lucy's hand across the table. "I'm so glad you were not involved with that Felipe drug dealer. He got what is deserved: a chest full of bullets."

"Well, you know Stella. You live by the sword—you die by the sword." Lucy lifted her glass. A natural smile came over her face, "Stella, I'm so happy you came."

The End

AUTHOR'S NOTE

I LOVE TO WRITE, and I love to hear from my readers. If you enjoyed this book or any of my others, send me an email, and I will respond

Get Vito Zuppardo's Starter Library FREE

www.vitozuppardobooks.com/newsletter

Vito Zuppardo is the author of 16 novels set in his history-filled hometown of New Orleans. He wrote and released his first novel, Alluring Lady Luck, in 2010 after spending 25 years in the casino business.

In 2011 Tales of Lady Luck, another well-received book based on actual events, dug deeper into the characters found on exclusive VIP lists, high-stakes gaming party jets, and in casinos worldwide.

After the success of his first two novels, Vito turned his attention to writing thrillers, and the first novel in the series, True Blue Detective, was a hit. A spinoff series called Voodoo Lucy soon followed.

Vito was born and raised in New Orleans and moved to Baton Rouge after Hurricane Katrina. It's his life adventures that make his books fun to read, and his characters stand out.

Life is what you make of it.

Connect with Vito via: Facebook (Vito Zuppardo Books), Instagram, BookBub, and Tiktok.

ENJOYED THIS BOOK? YOU CAN MAKE A DIFFERENCE.

Reviews are the most powerful tools in my arsenal for getting attention for my books. A committed and loyal bunch of readers. And I thank each and every one of you.

If you've enjoyed this book, I would be very grateful if you could spend just a few minutes leaving a review (it can be as short as you like) on the book's page.

Honest reviews of my book help bring them to the attention of other readers.

Please leave a review for "Night Terrors."

Thank you very much.

CHAPTER ONE

Present Day

THE FRENCH QUARTER NEVER slept. Jazz music wafted out of clubs until the first sign of morning, to be replaced by the much less agreeable clanks and screeches of a garbage truck picking up trash in the alleyway that separated Bourbon and Royal. One side of the alley was lined with trash cans from some of the hottest nightclubs on Bourbon Street, the other with mostly boxes from the art galleries that faced Royal Street. The sanitation truck was a block away, and with a hydraulic whine, the truck crushed cans, bottles, and boxes into its steel belly.

"Anything you'd like to say?" Lucy asked. Her real name was Lucinda Jones, but some called her Ms. Lucy. To street punks like Picklehead, who seemed to be struggling to process her question, she was known as Voodoo Lucy. In truth, she had several names. The one she used at any moment depended on what con she was running.

Lying on a flat cart used to move heavy furniture, Picklehead glared up at her, his head tightly held by a donkey harness attached to the handles of the steel cart.

"Well?" she asked, pressing on his neck with her foot.

"Yeah, I've got something to say—you're a dead bitch."

Lucy smiled at Picklehead. He was blinking rapidly, and he had a grayish cast to his face. He must have been coming down from his big rush, something he'd enjoyed only a short time ago.

"Didn't that little hit of coke take the edge off?"

With a look that could kill, Picklehead asked, "What do you want?"

"You can't take advantage of women," Lucy said, grinding her teeth until her jaw tightened. "Woman, teenage girls, and boys, you're not particular." She bent down and got eye to eye with him. "Not without consequences."

Standing in front of the cart staring at Picklehead, Lucy wondered what made people do such horrible things. The truck's brakes squealed as it stopped in the alley near the furniture shop's door. Shortly after, as she expected, the truck's hydraulics kicked in, the crusher's noise deafening. That was the sound she was waiting for.

Lucy pulled a syringe from her pocket, checked for an air bubble, and plunged it into his arm. Picklehead let out a scream and then another, only to be drowned out by the sound of the truck's hydraulics, which lasted for twenty seconds. By the time the clatter stopped, so had Picklehead's heart. The sound of the truck receded as it rumbled down the next block.

Her heart beating fast, Lucy eyeballed the alleyway, then pushed the cart carrying Picklehead out to it. Stripping off the harness and flipping his body to the ground, she propped him against a building. Working quickly, she placed Picklehead's thumb on the syringe, with the needle pushed into his arm. His hand dropped to the ground, the needle dangling from his skin as if Picklehead had squeezed every last ounce of juice from the syringe.

With the furniture cart cleaned of fingerprints and rolled back into place as if it had never moved, Voodoo Lucy walked through the building and out the front door to Royal Street, taking her usual seat at Café Beignet. Now it was a waiting game to see how long it would take for someone to discover what appeared to be another junkie overdosed in an alley.

CHAPTER TWO

Two months ago

LUCINDA JONES ALWAYS WALKED the streets of New Orleans with mixed feelings. Whispers of "Voodoo Lucy" reached her ears from the gossips as she passed. Others worshipped her as a goddess, calling her "Ms. Lucy," and were proud to be her friend. She stood five feet, nine inches with flawless skin, beautiful blue eyes, and natural red hair. Lucy attracted men without trying, even though applying makeup wasn't on her daily agenda. A colorful bandana over her hair was her signature look as well as floppy clothes covering her shapely body.

The legend of Voodoo Lucy had started eight months ago, shortly after twenty-eight-year-old Lucy and her mother Wanda arrived in New Orleans. Lucy had taken a part-time job at Bluff Salon, where her mother had also obtained employment as a beautician. The two received small salaries, decent tips, and free lodging in a tiny apartment above the salon on Royal Street. It was the new start they had hoped New Orleans could offer.

Lucy's father had lingered back in Tupelo, Mississippi, to sell off the few possessions that remained after they'd been evicted from their home. Tupelo had nothing for them but memories they all wanted to forget. Her father was supposed to join them within a week, but Lucy had said her goodbyes before leaving. She'd seen it in his eyes—he'd had no plans to meet up with them. After a month of waiting, her mother had finally given up and admitted to Lucy that she'd been right.

Keeping the salon clean was Lucy's job, along with fetching cold drinks from the vending machine or cups of coffee for customers. While sweeping up, Lucy frequently found herself drawn to the hair clippings that dropped to the floor. She kept the floor clean but would always save some red, blond, and jet-black hair in a bag. Why? She didn't know. Maybe it was their color or their texture that called out to her, but something about them was intriguing.

The French Quarter of New Orleans was home to many quirky people who kept odd hours and the salon wasn't a nine-to-five type business. Club dancers made hair appointments at nine at night so they could leave and go straight to work. Men working the doors at clubs and bars wanted their hair cut after work—and the clubs closed at five in the morning. Vivien Bluff, the owner, didn't turn any appointments down, and Lucy and Wanda soon learned why the job came with living quarters above the salon. They were open practically twenty-four hours a day, six days a week.

After a few weeks, Lucy caught on to specific repetitive interactions that customers had with the salon as well as with Vivien. She was a strange woman and a self-proclaimed psychic reader who had several regular customers and the occasional tourist. Her office was separated from the salon by nothing more than a long bead drape hanging from the ceiling where she sat at a table with an empty chair across from her and flipped through tarot cards most of the day.

Lucy often studied Vivien's psychic readings. Her clients blurted out their fears behind the bead drape like the area was soundproofed. They mostly told her their worries and Vivien read their cards, saying what could happen if they continued on their current paths. Her pronouncements weren't anything the clients didn't already know; they just wanted to hear it from someone else. Vivien was nothing more than a twenty-dollar-an-hour psychologist, calculatedly playing on their emotions and behavior from the minute they walked into the salon.

The night callers were men, mostly middle-aged, well-dressed and well-groomed. Vivien would sit with them and talk while they sipped on Hennessy cognac, something she offered her preferred clients. It was always the same routine. A few minutes at the table, then she gave the cue by rising with her glass. Her night caller responded by standing and leaving an envelope on the table. Then, with a drink in hand, he followed Vivien to a door she held open.

Lucy would watch each night from her perch on the top step of the stairway as the men smiled and gave Vivien a kiss on the cheek before walking into one of the bedrooms. Vivien would then return to the table, picked up the envelope, and continue sipping her cognac.

Lucy's ears would then focus on the whispers coming from the bedroom. It was always a woman's voice she heard, followed by a faint sensual moaning that would grow louder and more forceful—then it would be suddenly muted and all Lucy could hear from downstairs was Vivien lighting up a cigarette. Holding her breath, Lucy would wait until the act was completed and the door from the bedroom leading out to the alleyway was closed gently. Almost simultaneously, another well-dressed man would walk through the Royal Street front door, take a seat with Vivien, and be offered cognac in a fancy glass.

Not all the visitors were men, some were women. There were scary ones, too, and Lucy would hide in the rear room pretending to keep busy when they came calling. Every Wednesday afternoon, a man showed up like clockwork. Dressed in his traditional gang colors and draped in gold chains, he was an intimidating sight. Lucy noticed one odd thing about him: a butterfly tattoo on his thumb.

Whenever the man arrived, Vivien would summon a bold look for the salon workers and present the man with a smile and hand over one hundred dollars wrapped in a sheet of the morning newspaper. He'd take it from her as he roamed his hands over her body. He was a street thug with no respect toward anyone, much less a woman, the type of man Lucy had grown to hate as a teenager preyed upon by men. Behavior she'd hoped was limited to Tupelo, though that was obviously wishful thinking.

The way Vivien explained things, the exchange was the cost of doing business, and a small amount for the protection of her girls and night callers. She identified the man as Felipe Cruz of the Cornerview Gang. He would sometimes make his rounds with Felipe, Jr., securing his teenage son as next in line to lead. It was a criminal cycle that had been in place for decades, and Felipe was making sure the family business would continue.

Felipe offered that same "protection" to all the business owners in the area. The bartender who cut his whiskey with sugar water. The nightclub owner allowing his provocatively dressed ladies to join customers for drinks, charging the customer twice the price for drinks and the lady's company.

It didn't matter what your scam was; Felipe had seen it all. Serving to a lady what looked like booze but was nothing more than overpriced iced tea in a cocktail glass, better known as B drinking, or the most popular con by nightclub owners, taking an empty bottle of top-shelf whiskey and replacing it with rotgut. Most customers had no clue what they were drinking after their second drink. For a weekly on-time payment, Felipe protected you from any pissed-off customers, and his political connections would keep your business off law enforcement's radar. But that protection came at a price. Don't pay, and he'd report you to the federal agents at ATF or to the local police, or he'd just burn your place down.

Everyone paid Felipe Cruz.

But Lucy hadn't left Tupelo to end up under the thumb of another man who thought he could throw his weight around. Sooner or later, she'd find a way to handle Felipe Cruz.

CHAPTER 1

It was the early hours of the morning when the garage doors opened. The signature headlights of Dr. Walter Ross's Audi A8 shone brightly as he pulled the car out of the garage. He drove the car around the courtyard, stopping in front of the electric iron gates. The custom-made gates could be seen even in the darkness of night by the brightly painted gold arrowheads on top, an elegance people used to symbolize the wealth of the owner.

His Royal Street home was one of the few with such a stately appearance. In the world-famous New Orleans French Quarter, it was just a few blocks from hotels, antique shops, and restaurants in an area most people desired to live, but just simply couldn't afford.

He turned out of the drive onto Royal Street, and within seconds, the taillights faded into the night. Very few cars were on the road this early in the morning heading east, making it a quick trip to the airport. The New Orleans airport, on the east side of the city, is backed up against Lake Pontchartrain.

Governor Huey Long approved the construction of the airport in the mid-1930s on a human-made peninsula dredged by the Orleans Levee Board. During World War II, the airfield was used by the United States Air Force and housed the Tropical Weather School. The private airport, converted years ago, is seldom used, but it's an airport that Dr. Ross was always happy to visit no matter what time of day.

He pulled into the empty airport parking lot and drove around to the back, an area most people had access to only with the proper identification. Stopping at the security gatehouse, he put his window down and handed his ID to the guard on duty. A fat, plain envelope with twenty-five, crisp, one-hundred-dollar bills was all the identification he needed.

"Good morning, Dr. Ross."

"Good morning. I was never here. No log book, okay?"

"No problem, sir. Tarmac three is where the plane will park," the guard said, putting the envelope in his coat pocket. "The plane is on approach."

The security gate opened, and he drove to the end of the driveway. Dr. Ross stopped the car and took a black box out of the trunk. Carrying it to the front of the car, he stood, trying to see the Gulfstream III jet approaching the runway. He could hear the engines and see the running lights, but it was still too dark to see the aircraft. The airstrip stretched one mile out into Lake Pontchartrain, and pilots best be on their A-game when landing or they would find themselves and the plane at the bottom of the lake.

The airplane wheels came down, preparing for landing. The nose of the plane tilted up, and it looked like it was going into the water. While the jet was still over the lake, he could hear the engines roar as the pilot gave full throttle to thrust the plane down to the runway for a perfect landing. It taxied to the edge of tarmac three.

The plane came to a complete stop. The engines were shut down, and the electric stairs descended, gently resting on the ground. The aircraft was pure luxury and could only be afforded by the wealthy.

The cabin door opened, and two men appeared at the top of the stairs. It was evident they were of Arab descent with their shiny, dark skin, looking like they were just greased with suntan oil. They stood at the top of the stairs and made it obvious they were there to protect and serve their boss as they put their hands in their pockets and pulled back their jackets, exposing the firearms strapped to their bodies.

"Dr. Ross?" one man asked with a thick accent.

"Yes?"

"Please, come up. Raphael will see you now."

Dr. Ross slowly climbed the stairs, balancing the box in his hands. "Gentlemen, do you have my money?" he asked as one man took the package from him at the top of the stairs.

A tall, tan man came from the back of the airplane.

"Raphael?" Dr. Ross asked.

"Yes, I am. Will I damage anything if I open the box?" Raphael asked.

"No. Just don't break the clear seal. The box is refrigerated to the proper temperature," Dr. Ross said.

One man held the box while Raphael opened it. "One heart and two kidneys. How much time do we have?"

Dr. Ross brushed his fingers across the plastic seal once again, making sure it was airtight. "The organs should be transplanted within twelve to fourteen hours for best results."

"No problem, this plane will get us to South America in two hours. Your money is inside," Raphael said, handing Dr. Ross a small leather bag. Out of curiosity, Dr. Ross opened the bag and looked inside.

"It's all there, two hundred and fifty thousand. We must go. Thank you, my friend," Raphael said as they shook hands.

"Tell Amir I said hello, and I look forward to seeing him soon," Dr. Ross said as he stepped off the airplane. Raphael nodded his head, acknowledging he would tell Amir.

It took longer to drive to the airport than the entire transaction took. Dr. Ross walked to his car as he heard the electric steps of the jet being pulled up and the engine start. That quickly, the plane was ready for takeoff.

He put the leather bag of money in the trunk of the car. Then he quickly counted twenty-five bundles, making it two hundred and fifty thousand dollars.

A smile came across his face as he started the car engine and drove around to the gatehouse. As he waited for the gates to open, the guard gave him a gesture of thanks for the money he received for his silence. The only information logged into the record books was a refueling stop for a Gulfstream III at 5:49 a.m.

Dr. Ross sat in his car and listened to the roar of the jet engines rushing down the runway. It was only seconds before the aircraft lifted off the ground and flew over the parking lot, gaining altitude quickly as the airplane passed through clouds, breaking into the early morning sky. It hurried through the sky with an ice chest of donated organs for a happy recipient, somewhere patiently waiting.

These transactions had become a common practice for Dr. Ross. He forgot the professional oath he took, much less the fact that it was illegal, morally wrong, and broke every ethical principle. Selling human organs to the highest bidder on the black market had become a way of life. He was a physician who just didn't care about people; it was all about the money. He adjusted his Rolex watch, and he could see it was time to get to the hospital and make his rounds.

CHAPTER 2

Doris Bell took another deep breath and slowly exhaled. She looked around the room at all her get-well cards taped to her mirror, and the vase on her nightstand that once had fresh flowers blooming, adding some joy to her life and her room.

Time had passed, but little had changed for Doris, other than her health. She was born in a big, white, two-story stucco house on Wilson Drive over seventy-five years ago, in a beautiful area called City Park, just a few blocks from Bayou St. John. As a child, Doris and her sister would walk to the park and climb the oak tree. Spanish moss hung from the tree's limbs. The tree had to be over seventy-five years old, based on the size of the trunk.

The girls would climb as high as they could, then walk down the large branches that draped from the middle of the tree down to the ground. It was what most children did repeatedly for hours at a time to entertain themselves back in those days. Now, some sixty years later, Doris found herself back in the same home. It had been sold and converted to a retirement community.

It was called Riverside Inn, or as Doris called it, a place to wait for the calling.

Over the years, Riverside Inn expanded by purchasing homes surrounding the property. Some homes turned into gardens with trees, fountains, and walking paths. It gave everyone outdoor space in a tranquil surrounding. Doris took another deep breath. It was getting harder and harder to get air into her lungs.

"Are you okay, Mrs. Bell?" the volunteer sitter asked as she got up from her seat tucked away in a dark corner of the room.

Doris raised her hand for her to stop, as if to say—I'm all right, leave me alone. Doris never liked to be waited on, not at this point of her illness. She was given a sedative and could hear people talking in the hallway as she drifted in and out of light sleep. To her, the noise in the hall sounded like years ago when her brothers would fight in the stairwell.

The only thing missing was the ear-piercing voice of her mother yelling for them to calm down.

Christie Hampton, the only RN nurse on duty, walked into Doris's room, checked her blood pressure, and looked at her urine output. She followed the tube in Doris down to the large bag attached to the side of the bed to assess any problems. While the tube looked fine, there just wasn't any output, indicating her kidneys had failed. There was little more that could be done for Doris, even if she was in a hospital.

Riverside Inn was not a hospital, but a home for the elderly. The staff would take care of almost any medical problem, other than surgery. Most people came here to recuperate from a hospital stay and then were released. Others came because they were getting older, and their families could afford for them to get the best care while they were still enjoying life.

"Mrs. Doris, I'm going to give you something to make you relax," Christie said, shooting a syringe full of fluid into the port attached to Doris's arm. The port had been there for weeks.

Doris waved for Christie to get closer so she could whisper to her. Christie emptied all the liquid into the port and leaned in closer to her face.

"Do you need something, Mrs. Doris?" Christie asked.

"Yes, kiss my ass! You have been killing me slowly for the last month with whatever is in that syringe. You think I don't know what you are doing to me," Doris said with hatred in her eyes, motioning for her to get even closer. "Burn in hell, bitch."

Christie left the room, shaken by Doris's words, but knew it wasn't uncommon for someone on their deathbed to spew out their thoughts in a delusional state of mind.

She took a break, going to the usual place everyone went to get away, the front balcony, looking out at Bayou St. John. Except for the occasional police siren from a distance, it was a quiet place. Downtown New Orleans had turned into a battleground for drug dealers and prostitution, and in the quiet night, she could hear the sirens miles away. Times had changed, and this was a big difference from the glamorous days when Doris Bell was a teenager. She had told the story often to the staff, so much that the younger personnel thought she was just an old, feeble lady talking out of her head.

Doris would tell them that those were the days when people took pride in the way they looked and dressed. Women wore dresses with hats and gloves, and men wore suits and ties, just to go shopping or to a movie. That was when downtown businesses were thriving, and the movie theater was the place to be seen. Like most major cities nowadays, the downtown business districts had turned into nothing more than discount T-shirt and camera stores. The fashion days of the big high-rise department stores and people putting on their Sunday best clothes for a day of shopping were long gone.

Jack Warren, the night shift manager, was in charge of all employees, including the medical personnel, even though he had no medical background. His only real interest seemed to be bodybuilding, based on his large, steroid-induced, muscular frame. He would always join Christie on the balcony for a break. Coworkers had often caught them kissing and getting a good look at Jack roaming his hands over every inch of Christie's thin-framed, perfect body. It was well-known throughout the home they had more than a working relationship. Jack made it known early on that when they were out on the balcony, they were to be left alone. Very few people would stand up to Jack and dispute his behavior. While it was not appropriate in the workplace, the staff tolerated it.

Christie was built like an aerobics instructor and wore her clothes two sizes too small. It showed her shapely assets and that was all that was needed to get Jack's attention.

"Doris will not make it through the night," Christie said.

"We never expected her to last this long. If you had done your job, she would have been dead weeks ago," Jack replied.

"That's a little cold," Christie said, lifting her head from Jack's chest.

"That's life. She would have died soon anyway; we just need to rush it a little," Jack said with a slight smile, displaying that he enjoyed his power. "Do you have everything ready?"

"Yes," Christie said, escaping her job duties as a nurse by relaxing into Jack's arms. It would only last a few moments before she would be snapped back to reality and have to handle another person whose time had expired.

It was 3:10 in the morning, and the alarm at the night nurse desk went off. Someone was in distress. "Room one hundred four, Doris Bell," Christie said to the three night employees.

She rushed to Doris's room with one employee close to her side. As they hurried down the hall, people sleeping were concerned and peeked out their doors. "Everything is fine, go back to bed," Christie said, trying to make light of the problem.

All the house residents knew that sound too well. It was never good news when the alarm went off. Christie opened the door to Doris's room and quickly worked on her, but she could see she was gone. She did CPR on her while the aide set up the defibrillator, putting the paddles on Doris's chest.

"Clear," Christie said as she hit the button and Doris's body jumped off the mattress. She tried again. "Clear." It didn't revive Doris, and she was pronounced dead at 3:42 a.m.

The first call made was to Dr. Walter Ross, keeping with company policy. He was the president of the Ross Foundation, which owned Riverside Inn, and many other assisted living centers throughout Louisiana. He was the son of the famous Dr. Donald Ross, who developed the first successful organ transplant program in Louisiana and played a significant role in having organ donors sign up at hospitals. He was the dominant force in Louisiana who got the senator's approval to ask people to be a donor when a person renewed or got their first Louisiana driver's license.

There was no telling how many lives had been saved and improved through the organ donor program. Dr. Walter Ross was in complete control of the family fortune after his father died, though many said Walter could never fill his dad's shoes. His only sister never worked in the family business and was happy with her monthly inheritance check. It worked for her because neither of them could ever agree on anything.

Christie picked up the phone in Doris's room and dialed Dr. Ross's private number. He received the call on the second ring. "Dr. Ross, this is Christie from Riverside Inn. Mrs. Doris Bell has expired."

"I understand. You know what to do, just follow procedures," Dr. Ross said.

Christie quickly went into action and called the police and the house doctor, who followed procedures used on every death in the care center. Both the police and the house doctor arrived within a few minutes. They confirmed everything had been done to save Doris's life. Christie had done everything to the best of her ability, in a timely matter. The doctor and police signed off on the death certificate and gave her a copy.

All residents of Riverside Inn signed a donor form when they first arrived. Some knew about it; some didn't. So, Doris's body was sent to St. John Medical Center just a few blocks away and within an hour, her body was disassembled like a used car in a junkyard. Every healthy, human body part had a use and was properly prepared and put on hold until Dr. Ross arrived. He had his agenda; it didn't matter if someone was at the top of the list and this body part was a perfect match. The donated organs were in his control. At Riverside Inn, living was not an option. Residents were under Dr. Ross's control from the day they arrived, and to him, they were worth more dead than alive.

Made in the USA
Columbia, SC
11 July 2022